Welcome to this mon~~th~~'s ~~Harlequin Pres~~ents! At this festive time of year, why not bring some extra sparkle and passion to your life by relaxing with our brilliant books! For all of you who've been dying to read the next installment of THE ROYAL HOUSE OF NIROLI, the time has come! Robyn Donald continues the series with *The Prince's Forbidden Virgin,* where Rosa and Max struggle with their mutual—but dangerous—desire, until the truth about a scandal from the past may set them free.

Also this month, Julia James brings you *Bedded, or Wedded?* Lissa's life has too many complications, but she just can't resist ruthless Xavier's dark, lethal sexuality. In *The Greek Tycoon's Pregnant Wife* by Anne Mather, Demetri needs an heir, but before he divorces Jane, he'll make love to her one last time. In *The Demetrios Bridal Bargain* by Kim Lawrence, Mathieu wants a wife of convenience, and taming wild Rose into the marital bed will be his pleasure! Sharon Kendrick brings you *Italian Boss, Housekeeper Bride,* where Raffaele chooses his mousy housekeeper, Natasha, to be his pretend fiancée! If you need some help getting in the holiday mood, be sure not to miss the next two books! In *The Italian Billionaire's Christmas Miracle* by Catherine Spencer, Domenico knows unworldly Arlene isn't mistress material, but might she be suitable as his wife? And in *His Christmas Bride* by Helen Brooks, Zak is determined to claim vulnerable Blossom as his bride—by Christmas! Finally, fabulous new author Jennie Lucas brings you *The Greek Billionaire's Baby Revenge,* in which Nikos is furious when he discovers Anna's taken his son, so he vows to possess Anna and make her learn who's boss! Happy reading, and happy holidays from Harlequin Presents!

EXPECTING!

She's sexy,
successful...
and
PREGNANT!

Relax and enjoy our fabulous series about
couples whose passion ends in pregnancies...
sometimes unexpected!

Share the surprises, emotions, drama and
suspense as our parents-to-be come to terms
with the prospect of bringing a new baby
into the world. All will discover that the
business of making babies brings with it
the most special love of all....

Delivered only by Harlequin Presents®

Catherine Spencer

THE ITALIAN BILLIONAIRE'S CHRISTMAS MIRACLE

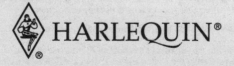

HARLEQUIN®

TORONTO • NEW YORK • LONDON
AMSTERDAM • PARIS • SYDNEY • HAMBURG
STOCKHOLM • ATHENS • TOKYO • MILAN • MADRID
PRAGUE • WARSAW • BUDAPEST • AUCKLAND

ISBN-13: 978-0-373-23452-3
ISBN-10:   0-373-23452-X

THE ITALIAN BILLIONAIRE'S CHRISTMAS MIRACLE

First North American Publication 2007.

www.eHarlequin.com

Printed in U.S.A.

All about the author...
Catherine Spencer

Some people know practically from birth that they're going to be writers. **CATHERINE SPENCER** wasn't one of them. Her first idea was to be a nun, which was clearly never going to work! A series of other choices followed. She considered becoming a veterinarian (but lacked the emotional stamina to deal with sick and injured animals), a hairdresser (until she overheated a curling iron and singed the hair off the top of her best friend's head, the day before her friend's first date), and a nurse (but that meant emptying bedpans!). As a last resort, she became a high school English teacher, and loved it.

Eventually, she married, had four children and always, always a dog or two or three. How can a house become a home without a dog? In time, the children grew up and moved out on their own and she returned to teaching. But a middle-aged restlessness overtook her, and she looked for a change of career.

What's an English teacher's area of expertise? Well, novels, among other things, and moody, brooding, unforgettable heroes: Heathcliff, Edward Fairfax Rochester, Romeo, Rhett Butler. Then there's that picky business of knowing how to punctuate and spell, and all those rules of grammar. They all pointed her in the same direction: toward breaking the rules every chance she got, and creating her own moody, brooding, unforgettable heroes. And that's where she happily resides now—in Harlequin Presents® novels, of course.

CHAPTER ONE

DOMENICO didn't usually involve himself with tourists. They were not, as a rule, vitally concerned with the wine industry except as it applied to their drinking habits. That morning, though, he happened to be crossing the yard to his office at the rear of the main building just as the latest batch of visitors filed from the vineyard toward the public section at the front. All but one headed straight for the tasting room. *She* remained outside, earnestly questioning his uncle Bruno who, at almost sixty, had forgotten more about viticulture than Domenico himself ever hoped to learn.

Although professional enough not to dismiss any question, regardless of how trivial it might be, Bruno was not one to suffer fools gladly. That he appeared as engrossed in the conversation as this visitor, was unusual enough for Domenico to stop and observe.

Tall, slender and rather plain, the woman

looked to be in her mid-twenties. And, he surmised, noting the slightly pink tint to her fair skin, newly arrived in Sardinia and not yet acclimatized to the sun. Unless she wanted to spend the rest of her holiday in bed with sunstroke, she should be wearing a hat. Tying up her hair in a careless ponytail that left her nape exposed was asking for trouble.

His uncle must have thought so, too, because he guided her to a bench set in the shade of a nearby oleander. More curious by the second, Domenico lingered just within earshot.

Catching sight of him, Bruno waved him over. "This is the man you talk with," he told the woman. "My nephew, first he speaks the good English to make better sense for you. More important, what he does not know about growing grapes and turning them into fine wine, it is not worth knowing."

"And my uncle never exaggerates," Domenico said, smiling at the woman. "Allow me to introduce myself, *signorina*."

She looked up and, for a moment, his usual urbanity deserted him. Suddenly bereft of speech, he found himself staring like a goatherd.

She was not beautiful, no. At least, not in the conventional sense. Her clothes were modest: a denim knee-length skirt, white short-sleeved cotton blouse and flat-heeled sandals. Her hair, though shiny as glass, was a nondescript brown, her hips narrow as a boy's, her breasts small. Nothing like the annoyingly persistent Ortensia Costanza, with her vibrantly dramatic good looks and ripe curves. If Ortensia exemplified blatant female sexuality at its most hungry, this delicate creature fell at the other end of the spectrum and almost shied away from him.

She was, he decided, the kind of woman a man could easily overlook—until he gazed into her large, lovely eyes, and found himself drowning in their luminous gray depths.

Recovering himself, he continued, "I'm Domenico Silvaggio d'Avalos. How may I help you?"

She rose from the bench with lithe grace, and offered her hand. Small and fine-boned, it was almost swallowed up by his. "Arlene Russell," she replied, her voice pleasantly modulated. "And if you can spare me half an hour, I'd love to pick your brain."

"You're interested in the wine industry?"

"More than interested." She allowed herself a quick, almost rueful smile. "I recently came into possession of a vineyard, you see, but it's in rather sad shape, and I need some advice on how to go about restoring it."

Smiling himself, he said, "You surely don't think that is something that can be dealt with in a few words, *signorina*?"

"Not in the least. But I'm committed to doing whatever I have to, to make a success of it, and since I have to start somewhere, what better place than here, where even a novice like me can recognize expertise when she sees it?"

"Spend an hour with the girl," his uncle muttered, reverting to Sardu, the language most often spoken on the island. "She is thirsty as a sponge for information, unlike those others whose only thirst is for the wine tastings they're now enjoying at our expense."

"I can't spare the time."

"Yes, you can spare the time! Invite her to lunch."

Her glance flitted between the two men. Although clearly not understanding their exchange, she correctly identified the irritation Domenico now showed on his face.

Her own mirroring utter disappointment, she murmured, "Please forgive me, Signor Silvaggio d'Avalos. I'm afraid I'm being very thoughtless and asking far too much of you." Then turning to his uncle, she rallied another smile. "Thank you for taking the time to speak with me, *signor*. You've been very kind."

As opposed to me, who's behaving like a world-class boor, Domenico thought, an unwelcome shaft of sympathy at her obvious dejection piercing his annoyance. "As it happens," he heard himself saying before he could change his mind, "I can spare you an hour or so before my afternoon appointments. I won't promise to address all your concerns in that time, but at least I can direct you to someone who will."

She wasn't deceived by his belated gallantry. Picking up the camera and notebook she'd left on the bench, she replied, "That's quite all right, *signor*. You've made it plain you have better things to do."

"I have to eat," he said, sizing up her too-slender length, "and from the looks of it, so do you. I suggest we make the most of the opportunity to kill two birds with one stone."

Although her pride struggled to fling his invitation back in his face, practicality overcame it. "Then I thank you again," she said stiffly. "I'm most grateful."

He took her elbow and turned her toward the Jeep parked next to the winery's huge rear double doors through which, soon, the harvested grapes would be brought for crushing. If she was nervous about hopping into a vehicle with a stranger, she hid it well, asking only, "Where are we going?"

"To my house, which lies a good five kilometers farther along the coast from here."

"Well, now I really feel I'm imposing! I assumed we'd eat in the winery's bistro."

"That is for the tourists."

"Which is what I am."

He put the Jeep in gear and started off along the paved road leading to his estate. "No, *signorina*. Today, you are my guest."

He was a master of understatement, Arlene decided.

She'd learned from the tourist brochures she'd collected that Vigna Silvaggio d'Avalos, a family-owned vineyard and winery going back three generations, was one of the best in Sardinia and that it boasted a prime location on the coast at the northern tip of the island, just west of Santa Teresa Gallura.

The elaborate coat of arms adorning the wrought-iron gates at the estate's entrance hadn't really surprised her. It, as well as the building whose handsome facade housed a state-of-the-art winery, tasting room, shop and garden bistro, were more or less what she expected of an operation touted as producing "internationally acclaimed wines of impeccable quality."

But when he drove through a second set of wrought-iron gates, and followed a long, winding driveway past what appeared to be private residences set in spacious grounds, to a pale stucco building perched above the beach, she was hard-pressed not to behave like the gauche tourist he undoubtedly took her to be, and stare open-mouthed. What he so casually referred to merely as his "house" struck her as being nothing less than palatial.

Screened from the others in the compound by an acre or more of gardens planted with lush, flowering vegetation, it rose from the landscape in a series of elegant angles and curves designed to take full advantage of the view. To the one side lay the breathtaking Smerelda Coast; to the other, acres of vineyards climbed up the hillside.

Escorting her through the main entrance hall to a wide covered veranda below which the sea shone green as the emerald for which it was so aptly named, he indicated a group of wicker arm-chairs upholstered with deep, comfortable cushions. "Have a seat and excuse me a moment while I take care of lunch."

"Please don't go to a lot of trouble," she protested, well aware that she'd already put him out enough for one day.

He smiled and retrieved a remote phone from its cradle on a side table. "It is no trouble. I'll order something to be brought down from the main house."

Well, of course he will, idiot! she reproached herself, reeling a little from the impact of that smile. Had she really imagined he'd disappear into the kitchen, don an apron and whip up something delectable with his own two hands? And did he have to be so unapologetically gorgeous that she could hardly think straight? Tall and dark, she might have expected and managed to deal with, but his startlingly blue eyes lent added allure to a face already blessed with more masculine beauty than any one man deserved.

After a brief conversation, he replaced the phone and busied himself at a built-in bar. "There, it is done. What would you like to drink?"

"Something long and cool, please," she said, fanning herself against a heat which wasn't altogether the fault of the weather.

He dropped ice into two tall crystal goblets, half-filled them with white wine he took from the bar refrigerator, and topped them off with a squirt of soda. "Vermentino made from our own grapes," he remarked, taking a seat beside her and clinking the rim of his glass gently against hers. "Refreshing and not too potent. So, Signorina Russell, how did you come by this vineyard you speak of?"

"I inherited it."

"When?"

"Just ten days ago."

"And it is here, on the island?"

"No. It's in Canada—I'm Canadian."

"I see."

But he obviously didn't. He quite plainly wondered what she was doing in Sardinia when her interests lay on the other side of the world.

"The thing is," she hastened to explain, before he decided she was just another dilettante not worth his time, "I'd already paid for my holiday here, and because this inheritance landed in my lap so unexpectedly, I thought it best not to rush into anything until I'd talked to a few experts of which, it turns out, there are many here in Sardinia. I've never been the rash, impulsive type, and now didn't seem a good time to start."

"You have no experience at all in viticulture, then?"

"None. I'm a legal secretary and live in Toronto. And to tell the truth, I'm still reeling from the news that I now own a house and several acres of vineyards in British Columbia—that's Canada's most western province, in case you don't know."

"I'm familiar with B.C.," he informed her tersely, as if even an infant still in diapers would have a thorough geographical knowledge of the world's second largest country. "Have you seen this place for yourself, or are you relying on secondhand information about its condition?"

"I spent a couple of days there last week."

"And what else did you learn, as a result?"

"Nothing except that it's very run-down—oh, and that an elderly manager-cum-overseer and two rescued greyhounds are part of my legacy."

He rolled his altogether gorgeous eyes, as if to say, *Why me, oh Lord?* "May I ask what you propose to do about them?"

"Well, I'm not about to abandon them, if that's what you're suggesting."

"I'm suggesting nothing of the sort, Signorina Russell. I'm merely trying to establish the extent of, for want of a better word, your 'undertaking.' For example, exactly how many acres of land do you now own?"

"Seven."

"And the kind of grapes grown there?"

"I don't know." Then, before he could throw up his hands in disgust and tell her to go bother someone else because she'd tried his patience far enough for one day, she added, "Signor Silvaggio d'Avalos, I realize this might be difficult for you to understand, growing up as you have, so surrounded by the business of cultivating grapes and turning them into wine that you probably started assimilating knowledge from the cradle, but I am a complete novice and although I'm willing to learn, I have to start somewhere, which is why I'm here with you, now."

He listened, his expression impassive. "And

you're very sure you have the stamina required to fulfill your ambitions, are you?" he inquired, when at last she stopped to draw breath.

"Very."

He regarded her, his gaze unnervingly intent. "Then if what you have told me is correct, I must warn you that even if you were an expert, you would be undertaking a project of massive proportion whose success is by no means guaranteed. And by your own admission, you are anything but expert."

"Well, I didn't expect it would be easy," she floundered, so mesmerized by his brilliantly blue eyes that it was all she could do to string two words together. "But I meant what I said. Succeeding in this venture is very important to me for all kinds of reasons, not the least of which is that there are others whose welfare depends on it. I am determined to go through with it, regardless of the difficulties it entails."

"Very well." He leaned one elbow on the arm of his chair and cradled his jaw in his hand. "In that case, take out your pen and let's get started on what you need to know at the outset."

In the half hour before their lunch arrived— cold Mediterranean lobster in a creamy wine sauce, avocado and tomato slices, and bread warm from the oven, followed by a fruit and cheese platter—she wrote rapidly, stopping every now and then to ask a question and trying hard to focus on the subject at hand.

Despite her best efforts, though, her mind wandered repeatedly. The questions he fielded from her were not those she most wished to ask. Whether or not she might have to rip out all her old vines and start over from scratch, which varietals she should plant in their place, how much it would cost and how long before she could expect to recoup her losses and make a profit, didn't seem nearly as engrossing as how he'd come by his very remarkable eyes, where he'd learned to speak such excellent English, how old he was, or if there was a special woman in his life.

Although she made copious notes of every critical scrap of information he tossed her way, her rebellious gaze repeatedly returned to his face. To the slight cleft in his chin, and the high slash of his cheekbones which seemed more Spanish than Italian. To the tawny sheen of his skin and his glossy black hair. To the dark sweeping elegance of his brows and the way his long, dense lashes so perfectly framed his vivid blue eyes.

"So, I have not managed to discourage you?" he inquired, as they sat down to the meal.

"You've made me aware of pitfalls I might not otherwise have recognized," she told him, choosing her words carefully, "but no, you have not discouraged me. If anything, I'm more determined than ever to bring my vineyard back to life."

He considered that for a moment, then said, "Tell me more about this great-uncle of yours. Why, for example, did he allow his vines to fail so drastically?"

"I suppose because he was too old to look after them properly. He was eighty-four when he died."

"You *suppose?* Were you not close to him during his lifetime?"

"No. I didn't even know of his existence until his lawyer contacted me regarding his estate."

"He had no other relatives? None better equipped than you to rescue his property from ruination?"

"I don't know."

"Why not?"

She stared at him, frustrated. *I'm supposed to be the one asking the questions, not you!* she felt like telling him. "Because he was from my father's side of the family."

"You did not care for your father and his kin?"

Kin. An old-fashioned word which, coupled with his charming accent, gave one of the few indications that English wasn't his mother tongue. "I barely knew my father," she said, wrenching her mind back to the matter at hand. "He died when I was seven."

He raised a lofty brow. "I remember many relatives and events from when I was that age."

"Probably because, unlike mine, your family stayed together."

"Your parents were divorced?"

"Oh, yes, and the war between them never ended," she said, remembering all too well her mother's vitriolic outpourings to Arlene's hesitant requests to visit her father or speak to him by phone. "I was four at the time, and my mother made sure I lived too far away from my father to see him often."

Domenico Silvaggio d'Avalos shook his head disapprovingly. "I cannot imagine such a thing. When a man and a woman have created a child together, his or her welfare comes before any thought of the parents' personal happiness."

"A fine philosophy in theory, *signor*, but not so easy to live by, I suspect, if the couple in question find themselves irreconcilably opposed to one another's wishes and needs."

"All the more reason to choose wisely in the first place then, wouldn't you say?"

She laughed. "You're obviously not married!"

"No," he said, and turned that unsettling gaze on her again. "Are you?"

"No. But I'm realistic enough to know that if ever I am, a wedding ring provides no guarantee that the marriage will last."

"I do not call that realistic," he said flatly. "I call it defeatist."

"Then that makes you an idealist who's more than a little out of touch with the rest of the world."

"Hardly," he replied. "My parents have been happily married for thirty-nine years, as were my grandparents for almost half a century. And I have four sisters, all blissfully happy in their marriages."

"But you're still single."

"Not because I have anything against marriage. My father's health isn't the best and I took over the running of this company sooner than I might otherwise have done, which has kept me fully occupied and left little time for serious romance. But I'll know the right woman when she comes along and I will commit to her for the rest of my life, regardless of whatever difficulties we might encounter— and they will be few, I assure. I'll make certain of that before putting a ring on her finger."

"You have a list of requirements she must meet, in order to qualify as your wife, do you?"

"Of course," he said, as if it were the most natural thing in the world. "Happiness, like sexual compatibility and physical attraction, will run secondary to suitability."

"You make it sound as if you believe in arranged marriages."

"I don't disbelieve in them."

"Then I pity the woman who becomes your wife."

It was his turn to laugh. "Pity yourself, *signorina*," he declared, tossing down his napkin. "You're the one willing to sell her soul to a lost cause."

"On the contrary, *signor*. I'm doing exactly as you claim you will, when you take a wife. I'm sticking with my decision, regardless of the difficulties I'm facing. The only difference is, I'm taking on a vineyard instead of a husband."

He regarded her for an interminably long, silent minute. Finally he said, "Well then, since you refuse to let me deter you, I suppose I must do all I can to assist you."

"I think you've already done that." She indicated her notebook. "You've given me some very valuable pointers."

"Theory is all very well in its place, *signorina*, but it in no way replaces hands-on experience. That being the case, I have a proposition which you might find interesting. One, I'd go so far as to say, you can't afford to refuse. I'll take you on as a short-term apprentice during your time here—say from eight in the morning until two in the afternoon. It will mean you spend a good portion of the day working instead of enjoying the usual tourist activities, but if you're as determined as you say you are—"

"Oh, I am!" she exclaimed, her attention split

evenly between the purely practical benefits of his offer, and the thrilling prospect of spending more time with him.

"Then here is what I suggest we do."

He proceeded to outline a course of instruction geared to get her started. That he was showing extraordinary generosity to a total stranger did not, of course, escape her notice, but Arlene couldn't help noticing not just *what* he said, but how he said it; on his finely carved lips as they shaped his words, and his precise enunciation.

Nor was that her only thought. He spoke with the passion of a true professional about the wine industry. Would he prove an equally passionate lover, she wondered.

"Signora?" His voice, deep and faintly amused, snapped her attention back to where it properly belonged. "Are we done for now, or is there something else you'd like to know?"

Nothing to do with viticulture, certainly!

"No, thank you." Flustered, she'd stuffed her notebook into her bag and pushed away from the table. A quick glance at her watch showed it was almost four o'clock. The two-hour lunch he'd promised her had lasted well into the afternoon. "My goodness, look at the time! I had no idea it was so late, and I do apologize. I'm afraid I've overstayed my welcome."

"Not at all," he replied smoothly, rising also.

She was tall, but he was taller. Well over six feet. Slim and toughly built, with a midriff as unyielding as a flatiron. A tailor's dream of a body, narrow in all the right places; broad and powerful where it should be.

Escorting her back to the Jeep, he inquired, "You have other plans for the rest of the day, do you?"

"Nothing specific. We arrived only yesterday and are still getting our bearings, but I should head back to the hotel."

"You did not come to Sardinia alone?"

"No."

"Then I am the one who must apologize for monopolizing so much of your time." He slammed her door shut, and climbed into the driver's seat. "Tomorrow the grape harvest begins, which means we'll be out in the fields all day. Wear sturdier shoes than those you presently have on. Also, choose clothing that'll give you some protection from the sun. You have very fair skin."

Fair? Beside him, she felt colorless. Insignificant. But that he'd noticed her at all would have left her glowing had he not concluded with, "In particular, make sure you wear a hat. Neither I nor anyone else working the vines needs the distraction of your fainting from heatstroke."

His obvious and sudden impatience to be rid of

her had quashed her romantic fantasies more effectively than a bucket of cold water thrown in her face. "Understood. You won't even know I'm there."

"You may be sure that I will, *signorina*," he replied with unflinching candor. "I shall be keeping a very close eye on you. You will learn as much as I can teach you in the short time at our disposal, but it will not be at the expense of my crop."

CHAPTER TWO

"SO THERE you have it. What do you think?"
Eyeing Gail, her best friend and travel companion, whom she'd found stretched out on a chaise by the hotel pool, Arlene tried to gauge her reaction to this abrupt change in plans.

"That he's right." Gail slathered on another layer of sunscreen. "It's a heaven-sent opportunity and you can't afford to turn it down."

"But it does interfere with our holiday."

"Not mine," Gail returned cheerfully. "We came here to unwind and I'm more than happy to spend half the day lazing here or on the beach. In case you haven't noticed, both are littered with gorgeous men, which is probably a lot more than can be said about what's-his-name from the vineyard."

"Domenico Silvaggio d'Avalos." Arlene let each exotic syllable roll off her tongue like cream, and thought that one glance at his aristocratic face and big, toned body would be enough to change

Gail's mind about which of them had stumbled across the better deal.

"What a mouthful! How do you wrap your tongue around it? Or are you on a first-name basis already?"

"Not at all. He's very businesslike and quite distant, in fact."

"Well, I don't suppose it really matters. Just as long as you leave here knowing a heck of a lot more about running a vineyard than you did when you arrived, he doesn't have to be witty or charismatic, does he?"

"No."

Arlene did her best to sound emphatic, but something in her tone must have struck a hollow note because Gail removed her sunglasses, the better to skewer her in a mistrustful gaze. "Uh-oh! What aren't you telling me?"

"Nothing," she insisted, not about to confess that, in the space of three hours, she'd almost fooled herself into believing she might have met Mr. Right. Gail would have laughed herself silly at the idea, and rightly so. There was no such thing as love at first sight, and although a teenager might be forgiven for believing otherwise, a woman pushing thirty was certainly old enough to know better. "I find him a little…unsettling, that's all."

"Unsettling how?"

She aimed for a casual shrug. "I don't know. Maybe 'intimidating' is a better word. He's larger than life somehow, and so confidently in charge of himself and everything around him. I don't quite know why he's bothering with an ignoramus like me, and I guess I'm afraid I'll disappoint him."

"So what if you do? Why do you care what he thinks?"

Why? Because never before had she felt as alive as she did during the time she'd spent with him. "His mood changed, there at the end," she said wistfully. "I could hear it in his voice and see it in his expression, as if he suddenly regretted his invitation. He seemed almost angry with me, although I can't imagine why."

Gail popped her sunglasses back in place and turned her face up to the sun. "Arlene, do yourself a favor and stop analyzing the guy. Bad-tempered and moody he might be, but as far as you're concerned, he's the means to an end, and that's all that matters. Once we leave here, you'll never have to see him again."

She was unquestionably right, Arlene decided, and wished she could find some comfort in that thought. Instead it left her feeling oddly depressed.

That night at dinner in the main house, the reaction of his brothers-in-law to what he'd done was pretty much what he expected. Mock disgust and a host of humorous comments along the lines of, "Where do you find these lame ducks, Dom?" and, "Just what we need at the busiest time of the year—the distraction of a useless extra female body cluttering up the landscape!"

His sisters, though, twittered like drunken sparrows, clamoring for more personal information.

"What's her name?"

"Is she pretty?"

"Is she single?"

"How old is she?"

"Don't just sit there looking stony-faced, Domenico! Tell us what makes her so special."

"What makes her special," his uncle Bruno declared, stirring up another flurry of over-the-top excitement, "is that she could be The One. Trust me. I have seen her. She is lovely."

The squeals of delight *that* comment elicited were enough to make him want to head for the hills. His mother and sisters' chief mission in life was to see him married, and the last thing they needed was Bruno or anyone else encouraging them. "Don't be ridiculous, Uncle Bruno," he snapped. "She's just an ordinary woman in the extraordinary position of finding herself with a vineyard she hasn't the first idea how to manage. I'd have made the same offer if she'd been a man."

But she wasn't a man, and no one was more conscious of that fact than Domenico. Throughout their extended lunch, he'd been struck by the sharp intelligence in her lovely gray eyes. But it took more than brains to succeed in viticulture, and given her small, delicate bones, he wondered how she'd begin to survive the tough physical demands of working a vineyard.

Not my concern, he'd told himself, more than once. Yet he admired her determination and he'd enjoyed their spirited debate on marriage, enough that he'd been tempted to ask her out to dinner, just for the pleasure of getting to know her better. Until she let slip that she hadn't come to the island alone, that was—and then he'd felt like a fool for not having figured it out for himself. If she was not a raving beauty, nor was she as plain as he'd first supposed. Rather, she possessed a low-key elegance of form and face that any discerning man would find attractive.

Too bad another had already staked a claim to her, he'd thought at the time, covering his irritation with a brusqueness he now regretted. She'd almost flinched at his tone, as he spelled out what he expected of her when she showed up tomorrow morning. If it weren't that she was in such dire straits, she'd probably have flung his generous offer of help back in his face. He would have, in her place.

Aware that his family continued to stare at him expectantly, he said, "At the risk of ruining your evening and dashing all hope of marrying me off before the last grape is picked, I feel compelled to point out that this woman is already spoken for. Not only that, she's here for only two weeks, after which our relationship, such as it is, will come to an end."

"But a great deal can happen in two weeks," Renata, his youngest sister, pointed out, ogling her husband. "Our honeymoon lasted only that long, but it was all the time we needed for me to become pregnant."

"Lucky you," Domenico replied testily, amid general laughter. "However, my ambitions with this woman run along somewhat different lines, so please don't start knitting little things on my behalf."

That gave rise to such hilarity that, so help him, if he'd known at which hotel Arlene Russell was staying, he'd have phoned and left a message saying something had come up and he'd had to cancel their arrangement.

Domenico Silvaggio d'Avalos was already directing operations when Arlene showed up as planned at the back of the winery, the next morning. Stepping away from a crowd of about thirty men and women being loaded into the back of two trucks, he eyed her critically, then gave a brief nod of approval. "You'll do," he decided.

"What a relief, *signor!*"

Either he didn't pick up on her lightly sugared sarcasm, or he chose to ignore it. "Since we'll be working closely for the next several days," he announced briskly, "we'll dispense with the formality. My name is Domenico."

"In that case, I'm Arlene."

"Yes, I remember," he said, rather cryptically she thought. "And now that we've got that settled, let's get moving. Those people you see in the trucks are extra pickers hired to help bring in the harvest. Stay out of their way. They have a job to do. If you have questions, ask me or my uncle."

She'd have saluted and barked, *Yes, sir!* if he'd given her half a chance. But he herded her into the Jeep and followed the two trucks up the hill to the fields, talking on his cell phone the entire time. When they arrived, his uncle was already assigning the extra laborers to their designated picking areas under the leadership of one of the full-time employees, but he stopped long enough to welcome Arlene with a big smile. "Watch and learn, then you go home the expert," he shouted cheerfully.

Hardly that, she thought. But hopefully not a complete nincompoop, either.

"Although some cultivators bring in machinery to get the job done quickly, we handpick our grapes," Domenico began, wasting no time launching into his first lecture.

"So I see. Why is that?"

"Because mechanical harvesters shake the fruit from the vines, often damaging it. This can result in oxidization and microbial activity which, in turn, causes disease. Not only that, it's virtually impossible to prevent other material also being collected, especially leaves."

Oxidization? Microbial? Whatever happened to plain, uncomplicated English?

Covering her dismay at already finding herself at a loss, she said, "But isn't handpicking labor intensive, and therefore more expensive?"

He cast her a lofty glance. "Vigna Silvaggio d'Avalos prides itself on the superiority of its wines. Cost is not a factor."

"Oh, I see!" she replied weakly, and properly chastised, wondered how she'd ever manage to redeem herself for such an unforgivable oversight.

Unfortunately her woes increased as the morning progressed. Although recognizing that she'd had the extreme good fortune to find herself involved in a world-class operation, what struck her most forcibly as the hours dragged by was that her back ached and the sun was enough to roast a person alive.

Under Domenico's tutelage, she picked clusters of grapes using a pair of shears shaped like pointed scissors. She learned to recognize unripe or diseased fruit, and to reject it. Because bruised grapes spoil easily, she handled the crop carefully, laying the collected clusters in one of many small buckets placed at intervals along each row.

Not that she'd have understood them anyway, but none of the migrant workers had much to say for themselves. They bent to their task with dogged persistence, seldom sparing her so much as a glance. Once assured that she wasn't about to lay devastation to his precious crop, Domenico essentially ignored her, too, and Bruno was too far away to offer her a word of encouragement. Over the course of the morning, however, four women found occasion to stop by separately, each offering a friendly greeting and, at the same time, subjecting her to a thorough and somewhat amused inspection. Even if they hadn't introduced themselves as his sisters, she'd have had to be blind not to see their resemblance to her mentor.

"Don't let my brother wear you out," Lara, the first to pay a visit, counseled, her English almost as flawless as Domenico's. "He's a slave driver, especially at harvest time. Tell him when you've had enough."

Not a chance! Arlene knew from the way

Domenico periodically came to check on her that he was just waiting for her to throw in the towel—which she would have done, if her pride had permitted it. But despite a dull, persistent ache above her left eye which grew steadily worse as the morning passed, she refused to give him the satisfaction.

The sun was high when a van rolled to a stop on a dusty patch of rocky ground some distance away from the fields. At once, the sisters converged on it and started unloading its contents onto a long table set up under a canvas awning supported by a steel frame.

As everyone else working the fields downed tools, Domenico approached Arlene. "Time for a break and something to eat," he declared, in that lordly take-it-or-leave-it manner of his.

By then, the pain in her head was so severe, starbursts of flashing light were exploding before her eyes and she wasn't sure she could crawl to where the women were laying out baskets of bread and platters laden with cheese, thinly sliced smoked meat and olives. But either he was blessed with second sight, or the stabbing agony showed on her face because, just when she feared she'd pass out, he grabbed her hand and hauled her to her feet. "Still want to run a vineyard?" he inquired smoothly.

"You bet," she managed, and disengaging

herself from his hold, managed to totter off and collapse in the shade of the awning.

Following, he eyed her critically. "How much water have you drunk since you got here?"

"Not enough, I guess." She squinted against the painfully bright glare of the sun beyond the awning. "I did bring a bottle with me, but I finished it hours ago."

"You didn't notice the coolers at the end of each row of vines? You didn't think to ask what they were for?"

"No." She swallowed, the smell of warm yeasty bread, olives and sharp cheese suddenly causing her stomach to churn unpleasantly.

He let fly with an impatient curse and strode to the table, returning a moment later to thrust at her another bottle of water, this one well chilled. "It didn't occur to me you'd need to be told to keep yourself properly hydrated. I assumed you had enough sense to reach that conclusion unaided."

Another of his sisters, this one well into pregnancy, happened to overhear him. "Domenico, please! Can you not see the poor woman has had enough for one day?" she chided, hurrying forward with a plate of food. "Here, *signorina*. I've brought you something to eat."

Arlene grimaced, by then so sick from the

pounding in her head that she was afraid to open her mouth to reply, in case she threw up instead.

With a sympathetic murmur, his sister lowered herself carefully to her knees. "You are in distress, *cara*. What can I do to help you?"

She tried to shrug away the woman's concern but, by then, even so small a movement was beyond her. "I have a bad headache here," she mumbled, pressing her hand to her temple, and hating herself for her weakness almost as much as she hated Domenico for witnessing it.

"More than just a headache, I think," his sister said, glancing up at him. "It is the *emicrania*, Domenico—the migraine. She needs to be looked after."

"I can see that, Renata," he snapped.

"Then drive her down to the house and let Momma take care of her."

"No!" Horrified by the idea, Arlene managed to subdue another wave of nausea long enough to articulate her objection without embarrassing herself.

Renata took ice from a cooler and wrapped it in one of the linen cloths lining the bread baskets. "Do you have a rented car, *cara*?" she asked, placing it gently at the base of Arlene's skull.

"Yes, but not here. My friend dropped me off this morning."

"Just as well, because you're in no shape to

drive." Once again, Domenico hoisted her to her feet, this time showing more care than he had before. *"Avanti!* Let's go."

"Go where?"

"I'm taking you back to your hotel before you pass out. I don't imagine your *friend* will appreciate having you flat on your back—at least, not in your present condition."

If she hadn't felt so lousy, she'd have challenged him on his last remark. Instead she submitted to being bundled into the Jeep, leaned her head against the back of the seat and closed her eyes.

To his credit, he drove carefully down the rutted track from the vineyard so as not to add to her discomfort, but when they reached the paved road, he wasted no time covering the miles into town. Beyond a terse, "Which hotel?" he mercifully made no other attempt at conversation.

Once arrived, he ignored the hotel's No Parking sign, stopped the vehicle right at the front door, and came around to help her alight. "What's your room number?"

By that point almost blind with pain, she sagged against his supporting arm. "Four twenty-two."

"You have a key card?"

"Yes." She fumbled without success in her tote.

He muttered indistinctly under his breath—something unflattering judging by his tone—

found the card himself, and hoisting her off her feet, strode past the doorman and across the lobby to the elevator just as its doors swished open and Gail emerged.

Stopping dead in her tracks, she let out a horrified gasp. "Heavens, Arlene, what happened? You look like the wrath of God!"

"Step aside, *per favore*," Domenico ordered, when she continued to block his entrance to the elevator. "I wish to take her to her room."

"Hold on a minute!" Gail replied, clearly not the least bit fazed by his autocratic manner. "You're not taking her anywhere without me."

"Indeed? And who are you?"

"Arlene's roommate."

"*You're* her friend?"

"*You're* her mentor?" she shot back, imitating his incredulous tone. "The one who's supposed to be teaching her everything there is to know about growing grapes?"

"I am."

"Well, congratulations! You're doing a fine job, bringing her home dead drunk in the middle of the day."

"I'm doing nothing of the sort!" he snapped. "What kind of man do you take me for?"

"You don't want to know!"

"Gail," Arlene protested weakly, "it's okay. I

have a headache, that's all, and just need to lie down until it passes."

Gail's face swam into her line of vision. "Sweetie, what kind of headache has you practically passing out?"

"A migraine," Domenico interjected on an irate breath. "Perhaps you've heard of it."

"Oh." Her tone suddenly less confrontational, Gail backed into the elevator. "I'm…um…sorry if I came on too strong. I'll help you get her upstairs."

"Close the shutters," Domenico instructed, when they reached the room. "I understand it helps to have the room darkened."

While Gail scurried to obey him, he lowered Arlene to the bed farthest from the window, then sat on the edge of the mattress and stroked a cool hand down her forehead. "Close your eyes, *cara*," he murmured, and even in the depths of her misery, the shift in his attitude was not lost on her. Whatever had given rise to that unspoken edge of hostility between them yesterday and which had continued into this morning, melted in the deep, soothing warmth of his voice.

"I've never seen her like this before," she heard Gail whisper from the other side of the bed. "Shouldn't we call for a doctor?"

"She doesn't usually suffer from migraines?"

"Not that I'm aware of, and if anyone would

know, I would. We've been best friends ever since college."

The mattress shifted slightly as he rose to his feet. "Stay with her and keep the ice pack at the back of her neck."

Panic lacing her voice, Gail hissed, "You're just dropping her off, then *leaving*? What if—?"

"I'll be back," he said, as his footsteps receded quietly over the tiled floor.

As soon as she heard the door click shut behind him, Arlene struggled to sit up. "Gail…? I think I'm going to be sick."

"Oh, cripes!" Gail slipped an arm around her shoulders and eased her to her feet. "Okay, sweetie, come on. I'll help you to the bathroom."

They made it with seconds to spare. Wrenching and horrible though it was while it lasted, vomiting seemed to ease the stabbing ferocity of the pain just a little.

After rinsing out her mouth and splashing cold water on her face, Arlene lay down on the bed again and managed a feeble smile. "Don't look so worried. I promise not to pull a repeat performance."

"I'm going to hold you to that," Gail said, crossing to peer through the peephole as a knock came at the door. "You just took ten years off my life. Now lie still and look pale and interesting. Your Sir Galahad's back, and he's not alone."

"How is she?" Domenico inquired, the minute he set foot in the room.

"About the same," Gail told him. "But she threw up while you were gone."

Oh, please! Arlene whimpered silently. *Haven't I suffered enough indignity for one day, without your sharing that with him?*

"Then it's as well I summoned professional help. This is Dr. Zaccardo," he added, as a middle-aged man with prematurely gray hair advanced to her bedside.

"It is as you suspected." After a brief examination and a few pertinent questions, the doctor stepped back from the bed and nodded so energetically at the other two that Arlene shuddered inside. "I will leave this medication with you," he continued, reaching into his medical bag for a small bottle. "See, please, that she takes two tablets immediately and, if necessary, two more at six, this evening. However, treatment now is such that a migraine is usually dispelled in a matter of hours. If she shows no improvement by nightfall, you will contact me, but I do not expect to hear from you. By tomorrow, she will be herself again. *Arrivederci, signor, signorine.*"

With that, he was gone as quickly as he'd arrived, leaving Arlene to deal only with Domenico who didn't seem disposed to leave with equal dispatch. Instead while Gail brought her two pills and a glass of water, he went to the desk and wrote something on the pad of paper supplied by the hotel.

"If you're concerned at all, you can reach me at any of these numbers, and this one is Dr. Zaccardo's," he told Gail. "Regardless, please call me this evening and let me know how she's doing."

"I'm sure she'll be fine."

"I want to hear from you anyway. You'll be staying with her, of course?"

"Of course."

"Until later, then."

The next time Arlene was aware of her surroundings, the room was completely dark except for the soft glow from a lamp next to the armchair by the window, where Gail sat reading.

Cautiously Arlene blinked. Dared to turn her head on the pillow. And let out a slow breath of relief. No flashing lights before her eyes. No stabbing pain above her left temple. Nothing, in fact, but a cool, delicious lassitude—and a gorgeous bouquet of pink roses on the coffee table, some distance away.

"You're awake!" Gail exclaimed softly, setting down her book and coming to the bed. "How're you feeling, sweetie?"

"Better," she said. "Much better. What time is it?"

"Just after eight. You slept for over six hours. Do you need more medication?"

She sat up carefully. "I don't think so. But I'd love some water."

"Sure." Gail plumped her pillows, then filled a glass from the carafe on the desk.

Arlene sipped it slowly, letting the slivers of ice linger a moment on her tongue, then slide down her throat.

"Well?" Gail watched her anxiously.

"So far, so good." She indicated the roses. "They're lovely, Gail, but you should've saved your money. I'm not going to die, after all."

"Oh, they're not from me! *He* sent them. They arrived a couple of hours ago. Here, see for yourself." She handed over a card, signed simply *Domenico*. "Not long on sentiment, is he?"

"Apparently not." Nevertheless, a sweet, ridiculous pleasure sang through Arlene's blood that he'd cared enough to send her flowers in the first place.

"Pretty good at dishing out orders, though. I suppose I'd better give him a call and let him know you're feeling better."

She retrieved the notepad from the desk, punched in one of the numbers he'd written down, and almost immediately began, "Hi, it's Gail Weaver.... Yes, I know what time it is.... Well I did, as soon as she woke up… Just now… Well, I will, if you'll stop interrupting and let me finish a sentence…! No, she says she doesn't need them…. Because she's a grown woman, Mr. Silvaggio de Whatever, which means she, and not you, gets to decide what she puts in her mouth…. I don't know. I'll ask her."

She held the phone at arm's length. "Do you feel up to talking to his lordship, Arlene?" she inquired, loud enough for half the people in the hotel to hear.

Arlene nodded, unable to keep a straight face. When was the last time anyone had spoken to him like that, she wondered.

"Hello, Domenico," she said, picking up the handset on the bedside table.

"I hear you're recovered." Seductive baritone verging on bass, his voice stroked sinfully against her ear and vibrated the length of her body. "I'm greatly relieved."

"Thank you, both for your concern and for the flowers. If a woman has to suffer a migraine, waking up to pink roses does make it a little easier to bear."

"I'm glad you're enjoying them."

A pause hummed along the line, which she took to mean the conversation was at an end. "Well, I'll say good night, then—"

He cut her off before she could finish. "Arlene, I

blame myself for what happened today. Expecting you to work as long as others who are used to our climate was unforgivable of me, and I apologize."

"There's no need. You heard my friend Gail, a moment ago. I'm a grown woman. I could, and should have spoken sooner. As it was, I put you to a great deal of trouble at a time when you've got your hands full with the harvest. It won't happen again."

"Are you saying you've changed your mind, and won't be returning to the vineyard?"

"Of course not. I'll be there tomorrow morning at eight—at least, I will unless you've changed *your* mind."

"Not at all," he said, his voice dropping almost to a purr. "Until tomorrow morning, then."

CHAPTER THREE

DESPITE her objections, Arlene spent the next four days in Domenico's office. With thick, white-washed plaster walls, stone floor, recessed windows and heavy beamed ceiling, it served both as a business center and a boardroom. At one end of the vast space stood a large desk, filing cabinets, and high-tech computer station and communications system, but she spent most of her time at the other end, seated beside him in comfortable club chairs at a handsome conference table.

"You're coddling me," she accused him, when he told her she wouldn't be helping with the harvest again. "You think I don't have what it takes to handle the job."

"On the contrary, I'm trying to give you as broad a base of information as possible in the short time at my disposal so that, when you take over your own property, you'll have a better idea of what your priorities should be. I suggest you let me decide the best way to go about doing that."

So it was that, with the door closed on the bustle of activity taking place outside, she studied slide shows illustrating various irrigation methods, ideal sun exposure, elevations, climate and soil conditions for growing grapes. She learned about different varietals and the importance of choosing those best suited to her particular location, as well as determining the trellising system to support them.

Domenico drew up spreadsheets itemizing general expenditures, and a calendar outlining a typical work year in a vineyard. He supplied her with catalogs and names of reputable companies she could call on when it came time to buy seedlings and equipment. Recommended videos she'd find helpful, online courses she could take, and offered advice on the kind of help she should hire.

Just when she thought she'd never begin to assimilate the mountain of facts he threw at her, he'd call a break and they'd help themselves from the thermos of coffee, which always waited on the serving bar separating the two halves of the room. Then it was back to work until around one o'clock, when the same van that delivered lunch to the field workers, stopped by, and the driver brought in a covered tray for the two of them.

Unlike the food prepared for the pickers, though, hers and Domenico's was more elaborate and served on colorful porcelain, with linen napkins and crested silverware.

On the fifth day, he took her back to the fields and showed her how to use a refractometer to measure the sugar content of the grapes. "One drop of juice is all you need for an immediate digital read-out," he explained, demonstrating. "Good wine is calibrated at a sugar level of 22BRIX."

"Bricks?"

"B-R-I-X," he amended, spelling it out for her.

She opened her ever-handy notebook. What's that?"

"The scale used by vintners to measure the sugar solution in the fruit."

"And what did you say this thing is called…?"

"A refractometer."

She examined the small, hand-held instrument more closely. "I think I might have seen one of these among the other equipment, when I went to visit my property, but it looked pretty old and beaten-up compared to this."

"Throw it out and buy another," he advised. "Accuracy is crucial when it comes to determining sugar content. You could lose an entire crop if you harvest too soon or leave the grapes on the vine too long. As the sugar content rises, so does the pH. Harvesting has to be timed to maximize sugar content while minimizing acidity."

To an outsider witnessing these sessions, it would have appeared to be all business between him and her. And indeed, where viticulture was concerned, it absolutely was. But underneath, something less tangible was at work. Without a single overt word or gesture, an invisible tension grew between them that had nothing to do with grapes or wine, and everything to do with the tacit awareness of a man and a woman separated from the rest of the world by a thick wooden door that shut out all sight and sound of other human interaction.

The faint scent of his aftershave, of her shampoo, permeated the air in mingled intimacy. His voice seemed to take on a deeper timbre when he addressed her. He turned her very ordinary name into an exotic three-syllabled caress. Ar-*lay*-na.

Sometimes, she'd glance up from diligently filling yet another page with notes, and catch him studying her so intently that heat raced through her blood as if she had a fever. Other times, he'd touch her, not necessarily on purpose and never intimately. Yet even the most accidental brushing of his hand against hers was enough to send tiny impulses of sensual awareness shooting up her arm.

Simply put, she was enthralled by him. By the authority with which he imparted knowledge, and his patience as he explained the complicated science of viticulture. By his intelligence and integrity.

The respect he generated among his employees impressed her deeply. Nor was it limited to those working close by. She'd soon realized that his holdings extended far beyond Sardinia's shores. He was, as his uncle once mentioned in passing, an international celebrity in his field.

Most of all, though, his evident devotion to his large family touched her where she was most vulnerable. As a lonely, unwanted child herself, she'd ached for the siblings that played so large a role in his life. Yet within that close family circle, he remained his own person. Independent, and confident in his masculinity, he exuded a charismatic charm unlike any other man she'd ever met. That he also happened to be blindingly handsome was merely the icing on a very delectable cake.

But however strong the intuition that told her he was equally attracted to her, once she was away from him, the uncertainty crept in. Possibly her imagination was leading her astray, spurred by the intimacy of just the two of them, alone for hours at a spell. What she took to be glances laden with an erotic subtext might simply be his way of giving her his undivided professional attention. For all she knew, the way he smiled at her, as if they shared something special and personal, could be the way he smiled at all women.

Was she the victim of her own wishful thinking? Or was there something…?

"There's something!" Gail assured her, when she confided her doubts to her friend. "I could've told you that, the night he phoned to see how you were feeling after the migraine. I was listening in to the conversation between the pair of you, remember?"

Laughing, Arlene said, "I recall your panting furiously after he hung up, and gulping down ice water straight from the carafe!"

"What else did you expect? Cripes, Arlene, talk about *steamy!* That man was so hot for you, I thought the phone was about to explode in my ear!"

"That's ridiculous! We'd met for the first time just the day before."

"Which, it would appear, is all the time it took. Admit it, kiddo. Just when you were ready to give up on men, you've finally met one who stirs your little heart to beat a whole lot faster."

"That doesn't mean he feels the same way about me."

"How do you know? Have you asked him?"

The very idea made her break out in a cold sweat. "I wouldn't dare."

"Why not? You know he's not married, so why

not just go with the flow and see where it leads? What do you have to lose?"

"His respect, for a start. And for all I know, he could be involved with someone else."

"Or he could be waiting for a sign of encouragement from you."

"What's the point of encouraging him, when we both know I'll be leaving here in another nine days?"

"The point is that you might be shutting the door on a rather glorious thing called love at first sight."

"I don't believe in that," she said stubbornly, all the while knowing she was deluding no one but herself.

Gail sighed, obviously exasperated. "There are hundreds of people in the world who do, and who prove it by living together happily ever after."

But there were couples who mistook sexual attraction and infatuation for the real thing, and lived to regret it, and she ought to know. She'd been the product of such a mistake—the only child of parents who hated each other by the time she was born.

I sacrificed myself and stayed with him because of you, her mother had reminded her often enough. *If I hadn't fallen pregnant, I'd have left him within six months of marrying him and saved myself five years of misery.*

"But if you're convinced it's not possible in your case," Gail continued, "then leave love out of the equation, and just live for the moment. As long as you're careful, holiday romance, with a little lust thrown in for good measure, never hurt anyone."

But Arlene had never been susceptible to lust, mostly because, until Domenico, she hadn't met a man who inspired it. "I don't believe in that, either," she said. "It's too risky."

Gail rolled her eyes. "This, from the woman who threw everything away to take on a broken-down vineyard, a couple of greyhounds and a crabby old man? Give me strength!"

Just as she was ready to leave on the Friday, Domenico asked her what plans she'd made for the weekend. "Because," he said, "if you're interested, I'll take you to visit some of the other vineyards on the island. It never hurts to get someone else's viewpoint. The more you see and the more people you talk to, the better off you'll be when you start working your own fields."

Knowing Gail had hooked up with a local tour guide who'd promised to take her scuba diving, Arlene accepted the invitation, and did her best to subdue the flush of pleasure riding up her neck. "Thank you! I'd like that very much."

"Then I'll pick you up around ten and we'll make a day of it."

Once back at the hotel, she agonized over what to wear. The sensible blouse and baggy pants that had been her standard uniform for most of the past week? The unflattering cotton sun hat that made her look like a wilted weed?

"Definitely not," Gail decided, when asked her opinion. "You're used to the sun now, and you've picked up a nice tan from lazing on the beach every afternoon. Book yourself into the hotel spa this afternoon and splurge—nails, facial, hair, the works. Heaven knows, you've earned it. Go glam, and let him see what he's been missing."

"Glam" had never been Arlene's forte, but the mirror told her Gail had a point. Not only had the sun given her skin a honey glow, it had painted pale blond streaks in her light brown hair.

Four hours later, she emerged from the spa, so buffed and polished her own mother wouldn't have known her.

Such a pity you're so plain, Arlene, she used to say, *but considering what you have to work with, there isn't much you can do about it.*

Until today, she'd have agreed. But not anymore. Nails painted a soft coral, skin shimmering like amber silk and hair expertly trimmed and enhanced by golden highlights, made a world of difference to the girl her mother had once dubbed "painfully drab."

Giddy over her transformation, she stopped by the boutique in the hotel lobby and found the perfect dress to go with her new look. Full skirted, with a fitted bodice held up by spaghetti straps, it was made of soft polished cotton the same deep turquoise as the sea.

"Perfect!" Gail agreed, inspecting the finished results. "You'll knock his socks off."

The thing was, Arlene wondered nervously, would she know what to do about it, if she succeeded?

He showed up right on time, driving not the Jeep, as she'd expected, but a sleek silver roadster. He wore pale gray trousers, a blue shirt open at the neck and black leather loafers, which even to her inexperienced eye were clearly handmade.

"You look very lovely, Arlene," he said, stepping out of the car to afford himself a head-to-toe inspection, "but your hair…" He fingered a strand and shook his head. "This will not do."

She stared at him, too disappointed to be offended. "You don't like it?"

"It is beautiful, and I won't be responsible for spoiling it."

With that, he disappeared into the hotel.

Turning to watch, she saw him enter the boutique, then emerge a couple of minutes later with a long white silk scarf. "For the wind," he explained, draping it over her head, then crossing the ends under her chin and tossing them over her shoulders. "There, now put on your sunglasses, and you'll look exactly the part—an international celebrity, leaving her yacht for the day to travel about the island incognito, with her chauffeur at the wheel of her car."

He was joking, of course. No one in his right mind would ever mistake Domenico Silvaggio d'Avalos for a lowly chauffeur, any more than she'd ever pass for a celebrity. Not even the chinos and boots he wore around the vineyard could disguise his aristocratic bearing, let alone the discreetly expensive clothes he had on now. His watch alone probably cost more than she earned in a month.

He ushered her into the car, and within minutes they'd left the town behind and were headed west along the coast toward Sassari, where they made their first stop. "This vineyard also grows the Vermentino grape as we do," he said, pulling up before a castellated building fronted by an enormous courtyard. "The owner, Santo Perrottas, and I went to school together in Rome, and have been good friends since we were boys."

That much was obvious from the warm welcome they received. Although not in the same class as Domenico, Santo was nonetheless a handsome, charming man. When he learned the reason for their visit, nothing would do but that Arlene sample his wine, not in the tasting room used by the public, but in a private garden screened by espaliered vines already turning color and stripped of their fruit.

"I've heard of British Columbian wines," he commented, as they sipped the straw-colored, aromatic Vermentino. "They have won gold medals in international competition, I understand."

"Not from grapes grown on my land, I'm afraid," she said ruefully. "I inherited a vineyard that's been neglected for some time."

"Then you're in good hands with Domenico. He is a true expert in the art of cultivating healthy vines. And you, my friend," he added, turning to Domenico with a wry grin, "how lucky are you, to have come across such a *bellezza*! Why could she not have turned up on my doorstep, instead of yours?"

"Why do you think? Because she's as smart as she is beautiful. And because you're married."

Arlene felt a blush creeping over her face. She wasn't used to such flattering attention. Not that they meant it, of course. They were just being polite and charming because that was expected of men who moved in the elevated stratum of society they frequented.

From Sassari, Domenico drove south, stopping at three other vineyards on the way, where they were again warmly welcomed and pressed to stay longer—for lunch, for dinner, for the night. But he refused each invitation, and for that, Arlene was glad. Although she appreciated the hospitality, he was an excellent teacher and much of what she heard and saw, she'd already learned at Vigna Silvaggio d'Avalos. The true pleasure of the day for her was seeing his island through his eyes as he pointed out ancient ruins and breathtaking scenery.

Shortly before one in the afternoon, he drove inland for several kilometers to a village perched on a wooded slope overlooking the Mediterranean. Leaving the car on the outskirts, they walked along winding streets so narrow, the sun barely penetrated between the houses, and it seemed to Arlene that people could reach out of their bedroom windows and shake hands with their neighbors across the way. In a tiny square shaded by palm trees, they ate lunch at an outdoor restaurant, and were on their way again within the hour.

They reached Oristano just after four, and after a quick tour of the town, headed north again, following seventy-five kilometers of magnificent coastline and arriving in Alghero, on the Coral Riviera, just as daylight faded. Even so, the beauty of the city was apparent.

"It is the jewel of northwest Sardinia, if not the entire island," Domenico told her, after they'd parked the car and were strolling through the cobbled streets of the medieval citadel. At that hour, the bars and restaurants were just coming alive after the afternoon lull, with people gathering in social groups at outdoor tables, to sip wine and exchange gossip. "If you had more time here, I would bring you back to enjoy the beach and see more of what the town has to offer. As it is, we'll have dinner here and enjoy together what's left of today."

If you had more time here.... It had become a frequent refrain, during the day. Rose quartz beaches, secluded coves, forested hills, silent olive groves, archaeological ruins and seldom traveled roads leading to the wild interior: they'd have been hers to discover with him, if only she had more time.

Instead she had to make do with this one glorious day of fleeting impressions. Of smiling glances and shared laughter. Of his hand clasping hers to prevent her stumbling over the uneven paving stones. Of the wind whipping the ends of her scarf like the tails of a kite, as the car sped along the dusty roads. Of the sun touching the square line of his jaw and throwing deep bronze shadows under his high cheekbones. Of the scent of myrtle and sea pine capturing her senses.

These were the memories she'd take with her to her new home in British Columbia; these and the knowledge he'd shared with her. Did he know how indelible an impression he'd made, she wondered, angling a covert gaze at him as he led her purposefully past wonderful old palazzos and churches to a restaurant with tables set out under a colonnaded terrace? Or that no matter how many years passed, she'd never forget him?

Street signs, she noticed, were in Italian and what she thought might be Spanish, but which turned out more accurately to be Catalan. "You're on the right track, though," Domenico said, after they were shown a table set with dramatic black linens, white votive candles in crystal holders and wineglasses with stems as slender as flower stalks. "Alghero is more Spanish than any other place in Sardinia. In fact, it's nicknamed 'Barcelonetta,' meaning Little Barcelona. Not so surprising, when you consider it lay under Aragonese rule for the better part of three hundred years, starting in the mid-fourteenth century."

"The first time I saw you, I thought *you* looked Spanish, except for your blue eyes" she admitted.

"Many Spaniards—Italians also, for that

matter—have blue eyes, so once again, your instincts were on target. My father's family came from northern Spain in the early 1880s. I'm told I resemble my great-great-grandfather."

"He must have been a very handsome man."

"*Grazie*. And to whom do you owe your looks, my lovely Arlene?"

"Oh, you don't have to say that," she protested, flushing. "I know I'm not very pretty."

He reached across the table and took both her hands in his. "Why do you do that, *cara*?" he asked gently. "Why do you turn away from the truth and try to hide your quiet beauty from the rest of the world? Are you ashamed of it?"

"Nothing like that," she said, her breath catching in her throat at the intensity of his gaze. "I'm not being coy or fishing for compliments. I just know mine's not the kind of face that would launch a thousand ships."

"And who convinced you of that? A man? A rogue who broke your heart and left you with no confidence to believe what is so plain to the rest of the world?"

"It was my mother," she said baldly.

He let out a soft exclamation of distress. "Why would a mother speak so to her child?"

"I think because I take after my father."

"Then trust me when I tell you that your father

also must be a most handsome man, as you surely realize."

"Not really. I hardly knew him."

"Ah, yes," he said. "Now I remember. Your parents divorced when you were very young, and he died shortly after. But you have no photographs of him?"

Her laugh emerged shockingly harsh. "My mother would never have permitted one in the house."

He lifted his glass and surveyed her silently a moment. "You might as well have been left an orphan," he finally commented.

In truth, that's how she'd often felt, but he was the first to put it in words. "I hope you know how lucky you are, to be part of such a united family."

He started to reply, then seemed to think better of it and reverted to his role of mentor, instead. "Tell me what you think of this wine?"

"I'm enjoying it."

"No, no, Arlene," he chided. "I expect better of you than that. Tell me what it is that makes it so enjoyable."

She squirmed in her seat. A connoisseur of wines she was not. She knew what she liked, but that's about as far as it went. "It's Vermentino."

"Not good enough! All you had to do to reach that conclusion is read the label."

"It's refreshing."

"And…? What do you notice about the finish?"

"It has nice legs?" she offered haltingly, tilting her glass.

He threw back his head and burst out laughing. "*Dio*, I have failed as a teacher! You'll have to come back for a second course of instruction."

Oh, if only! she thought, her heart seeming to swell in her breast as she feasted on the sight of him. On his flawless teeth, and the lush, downward sweep of his generous lashes. On his eyes, dark as sapphires in the candlelight. How could any woman be expected to keep her head around such a wealth of masculine beauty?

Sobering, he leaned toward her. "Try again, my lovely lady. Inhale the bouquet. Take a slow mouthful and let it acquaint itself with your palate."

Feeling horribly self-conscious, she complied.

"Well? Tell me what you discovered."

"It's light," she ventured. "Fruity—but not overpoweringly so. And…with a hint of almonds?"

"Exactly! The perfect accompaniment to the seafood platter I recommend we order as our main course."

The moon had risen by then, illuminating the ancient domes and towers of the city, and casting deep shadows in the square beyond the restaurant. With the votive candles flickering between them, she and Domenico lingered over a fabulous selection of scampi, crayfish and mussels, served with a salad and a basket of the delicious bread she'd come to expect from the island.

"You left room for dessert?" he inquired, when at last there was nothing left but empty shells and crumbs.

"Heavens, no!" she exclaimed on a sigh. "I'm literally stuffed to the gills!"

"Then we'll finish with something you've yet to experience," he declared, gesturing to their waiter. "So far, you know only the regular Vermentino, a young, slightly bitter wine, served ice cold. Now, you must try its cousin, the *liquorosa*, more aged, sweeter and not so chilled."

"I think I've had enough for one day." Two glasses of wine was pretty much her limit, and they'd already consumed an entire bottle with their meal. If she had anymore, she'd either wind up under the table or throwing herself at him.

"Relax, Arlene," he said gently. "It is not my intention to get you drunk, merely to extend the pleasure of this evening as long as possible."

"I'd have thought you'd had enough of me by now."

"You are mistaken."

Three words, simply spoken, that was all. Yet they intoxicated her beyond anything alcohol could hope to achieve. The candle flames swirled dizzily before her eyes. The blood surged heatedly through her veins. Clinging to her vanishing sanity, she began, "You know everything about me—"

"Not everything," he murmured. "The best, I suspect, is yet to come."

"The point is," she almost panted, "I know next to nothing about you, so now it's your turn to talk. Tell me about you."

"What would you like to know?"

"Your deepest, darkest secrets," she said, injecting a teasing note into her voice to disguise her inner turmoil.

Tell me you cheat on your income tax, that you're wanted by the police and have a prison record, that you're an inveterate womanizer... anything to bring me to my senses, please!

He looked long into her eyes. Set down his untouched wine. Rose from the table and held out an imperious hand. His own voice suddenly hoarse, he said, "Why bother to tell you, when actions speak so much louder than words?"

CHAPTER FOUR

ON THAT note, he walked her out of the citadel to where he'd left the roadster, drove past a marina in which the masts of million-dollar yachts reached for the stars, and followed a road through a pine forest to an isolated stretch of coast.

"At this very moment," he said, finally breaking his silence and drawing her onto the beach, "what I most want is to hold you in my arms and kiss you, here in this quiet place, with nothing but the sea and sky as witness."

"Why?" she asked him.

"Because, at this moment, I find you more desirable than any other woman I have known."

He ran his hands down her bare arms and, catching her hands, pulled her toward him. The heat of his body reached out to envelop her. The height and breadth of him blotted out the pale moonlight and sheltered her from the cool sea air. The strong, steady thump of his heart reassured her. She was safe with him. He would let nothing hurt her.

He stood close, imprinting her with the evidence of his arousal. His gaze seared her, stripping her to the bone. His breath winnowed over her face, taunting her. Not until he'd reduced her to mindless anticipation did he at last, and with excruciating slowness, lower his mouth to hers.

She didn't have to be an expert to recognize that, when it came to a kiss, he was. The very second his lips found hers, she was lost. Lost in a reality that exceeded all fantasy. Tossed in a storm of emotion that left her shaking. Caught up in a turbulent wanting that screamed for more…for everything he was willing to give her.

…*nothing wrong with a little lust, as long as you're careful,* Gail had said.

But "careful" had no place in Arlene's world just then. The only thing that ruled was hunger, and it raged at her without mercy. Her mouth softened beneath his, eager and willing to accept him into its heated depths. Her tongue engaged with his, instinctively understanding the ritualistic prelude to greater intimacy and signaling her acquiescence. She clung to him, threading her fingers through his hair. Whimpered softly, an inarticulate little sound beseeching him to take all of her.

He did not. Instead he dragged his mouth away

and stepped back, leaving the cool sea air to flow over her limbs and infiltrate her heart. "It grows late. I must take you home."

His abrupt mood swing almost flattened her. He didn't mean what he said. He couldn't, not when, just nanoseconds before, his body had broadcast a blatantly different story.

"No," she whispered, clinging to him. "I'm not afraid. I trust you, Domenico. You don't have to stop—"

"Yes, Arlene," he said flatly, his voice rough as the granite decomposition of the soil that produced his grapes. "Oh, yes, I do."

Despair welled up in her throat, colder than ice. She'd disappointed him. Been too clumsy, too eager, too…too *everything!* Humiliated, she spun away so that he wouldn't see the tears glimmering down her face, and started back to the car.

He kept pace with her. Held open her door. Without a word, he again draped the scarf over her bent head, then climbed into the driver's seat. One quick turn of the ignition key and the car roared to life, its headlights slicing through the dark to play on the densely packed trunks of the pine trees.

The drive from Alghero to the small town where she was staying was both mercifully long, and cruelly, short. The roadster swept in a wide arc to the forecourt of her hotel and stopped, all the while muttering impatiently as if it couldn't wait to be rid of her and on its way again.

She opened her door. Swung her legs to the pavement. "Thank you very much for a lovely day," she said over her shoulder, reciting the words like a child well-coached by her mother. "Thank you, too, for all your kind help. I'm most grateful. Goodbye."

His silence had continued throughout the journey from the beach, but at that, he finally spoke again. "Tomorrow…"

Three syllables only, they were enough to paralyze her in mid-flight. But she didn't turn. Didn't dare look at him. Hardly dared to breathe, let alone hope. "What about tomorrow?"

"Take the day off. Spend it with your friend. You've hardly seen her since you arrived."

Another, more vicious wave of disappointment swept over her. *And you've seen altogether too much of me and don't want to spend another minute in my company! Why don't you just come out and say what you mean, Domenico?*

His voice grazed the back of her neck, stilling her retort before she could air it. Seeped into her pores, electrifying her. "I'll pick you up later… eight o'clock…for dinner…something different from tonight."

Long after the car had growled away, its red

taillights swallowed up by the night, she stood immobile and forced herself to breathe. She didn't know what he'd meant by his cryptic remark about "something different," nor, at that moment, did she care. All that mattered was that it wasn't over between them, after all.

Storming into his villa, Domenico poured himself a *grappa* and paced the covered veranda outside his living room, cursing himself for being the king of all fools. The minute his mouth touched hers, he'd known kissing her was a mistake and that the kindest thing he could do was never see her again.

He'd told himself that over and over again, throughout the return trip to her hotel because, as he'd learned when he was still in his teens, smart men avoided involvement with women who didn't understand the rules of the game. And that Arlene hadn't a clue about them became apparent the minute his lips touched hers.

The passion he'd awoken in her with just one kiss had stunned him. He could have taken her, there on a public beach, and she would not have refused him.

I trust you…you don't have to stop, she'd said, her voice thick and urgent with need.

That he *had* stopped was scarcely to his credit. Sexually he desired her in every way a man could desire a woman. Even thinking of how she'd felt in his arms—soft, compliant, sweetly responsive—was enough to stir him to painful arousal. But that word "trust" had awoken in him the voice of conscience and it would not be silenced.

How was it, he'd found himself wondering, that a woman approaching thirty retained such willingness to believe in the goodness of others, when all she'd known as a child was rejection?

And there, in a nutshell, lay the real problem, because he would not, *could not*, be the one to reject her again. However much he might want it, and however mutually pleasurable it might be at the time, they would never make love because her tender heart would end up being badly bruised.

She wasn't the casual type. For her, intimacy would mean love and marriage—and he wasn't in the market for either. Best to avoid further hurt and end things with her now.

He knew exactly the words to say. Rehearsed them all the way back to the hotel until he had them down pat. *It's been a real pleasure, Arlene, but I've taught you as much as I can, so consider yourself free to enjoy the rest of your holiday. Goodbye and good luck!*

Kind, but final, leaving no room for misinterpretation.

She'd beaten him to it. Served up her little

farewell speech with perfect composure, and let him off the hook—or so he'd thought until he heard the confusion in her voice and saw how her chin quivered despite her best efforts to control it. Until he saw her walking away from him, her spine so stiff with pain and hard-won dignity that it undid all his good intentions.

Suddenly, without thought for the complications he was bringing down on himself, he'd blurted out an invitation he never saw coming. One that promised nothing but trouble he didn't need.

Dinner alone with her was out of the question. Candlelight and wine made for a dangerous combination. Throw in a little music, a little star-shine, the dark intimacy inside his car, and the end result was a recipe, if not for disaster, then for lasting regrets. Even he wasn't made of stone.

"You're bringing her for dinner?"

"Here?"

"With us?"

The squeals of excitement that greeted his announcement the next day would have put a screech owl to shame.

"Don't make something out of it that isn't there," he warned his mother and sisters grimly. "There's nothing serious going on here. She's just starting out in this business, that's all, and the more she talks to people whose entire lives revolve around a vineyard, the more she'll learn."

"We understand," they crowed, their ill-concealed glee giving the lie to their words. "You're just being a good friend. There's absolutely nothing else going on."

As he drove past the main house on his way to collect her, he saw through the lighted windows the hive of activity taking place inside, and knew he might as well have saved his breath. Nobody had believed a word he said.

Well, it was up to him to prove them all wrong. He'd keep the mood light. Hospitable but impersonal. Pleasant without being overly familiar. In other words, treat her exactly as he'd treat any other colleague.

He arrived a few minutes early and was waiting in the hotel lobby when she came out of the elevator. If, yesterday, she'd been pretty as a picture in her sea-green sundress, tonight she was a study in classic elegance. Instead of leaving her hair to flow loose around her face, she secured it at her nape with a black velvet bow. She wore a straight black ankle-length skirt, open-toed black sandals, a simple, long-sleeved white lace blouse and pearl studs at her ears.

"I forgot to return this to you," she said, handing him the scarf he'd bought for her.

He bent and dusted a kiss on her cheek. A big mistake. The faint trace of her perfume reminded him of the wild violets that grew on the island in spring, but the softness of her skin struck a more intimate note and put a dent in his resolve to keep his distance. "It's yours to keep, Arlene, but you won't need it tonight. I put the top up, on the car."

She trembled slightly under his touch as he guided her outside. "Where are you taking me this time?" she asked, as he drove away from the hotel and turned the car toward the west.

"To dinner with my family."

"Your *family?*" she echoed, clearly shocked.

"That's right. You've already met my uncle and sisters. Tonight, you'll meet the rest." *As in, parents, in-laws, nieces, nephews, dogs, cats and anyone else he could drag into the mix!*

"I see." He felt her thoughtful gray gaze turn on him. "Why?"

He hadn't anticipated that question and had to scramble for an answer that would neither mislead nor offend her. "Because…because being welcomed into someone's home is the best way to really get a feel for a foreign country. Hotels and such are fine in their place, but they don't paint a true picture of the culture."

In the light thrown by a passing street lamp, he saw a frown marred the smooth width of her forehead. "I think what you're really saying is that you feel sorry for me, and I have to tell you, I don't need your pity, Domenico."

Dio! He'd forgotten she was as perceptive as she was lovely. "Of all the feelings you arouse in me, Arlene, be assured that pity is not one of them. If that's the impression I gave you, then I chose my words badly, so let me put it this way: I'd like you to spend an evening with my family because I believe you'll enjoy it, and I know for a fact *they* are eager to meet you."

"Why?"

"Do you realize how often you ask me that?"

"I'm sorry if it annoys you."

"I didn't say it annoys me."

She lifted her shoulder in a delicate shrug. "Then answer the question."

So much for keeping things light and pleasant! Tension, brittle as spun glass, arced between them. "Because I like you," he said, the annoyance she'd accused him of suddenly becoming a fact. He wasn't used to being so easily outmaneuvered. "I like you very much. I admire your intelligence and your determination. To be sure, we haven't known each other more than a few days, but we share common interests and I look upon you as a friend. That's it, pure and simple. I have no ulterior motive. We Sards are hospitable people.

We welcome friends into our homes. Is that so very difficult for you to understand?"

"No," she said, in such a small, crushed voice that he swore silently for speaking to her so harshly. "I guess I'm being hypersensitive, and I apologize. I tend to react like this when I'm unsure of myself, and I don't mind admitting I'm finding the prospect of being paraded before your relatives rather daunting."

His anger died as swiftly as it had arisen. "You have nothing to worry about. You'll worm your way into their hearts with no trouble at all."

Just as you'll worm your way into mine, if I let you, he almost added.

A sobering thought. One best kept to himself.

She was a mess; a bundle of nerves. Overnight, she'd had time to consider his last-minute invitation, and it had left her fluctuating between elation and the unwelcome suspicion that he was merely being kind, just as he would be to a stray dog he found on the side of the road.

"Calm down," Gail had told her. "Stop looking for a hidden agenda that isn't there, and just enjoy the evening for what it is—a date with a sophisticated, handsome man who clearly enjoys your company."

"But what am I supposed to wear? 'Dinner'

could mean anything from a hamburger at a beachside fast-food outlet, to a five-course meal at a private club," she fretted.

"Assume it's the private club, but keep it simple, just in case you're wrong."

The trouble was, Arlene thought now, eyeing him furtively as he navigated the curves in the road, nothing to do with Domenico was simple. He was the most complex man she'd ever come across, and she'd known from the start that she was hopelessly out of her depth in trying to deal with him. Discovering she was about to take on the entire Silvaggio d'Avalos family as well was enough to give her the shudders.

"This is the main house where my parents live," he said, turning into a driveway and pulling up under the portico of a villa which, like his, exemplified wealthy good taste. "My sisters also have homes here, and so do I, as you already know, but we're spread out far enough not to get under each other's feet."

She wished they'd stayed spread out tonight. The house alone intimidated her, and never mind the couple who lived there, but when a manservant opened the door and she saw the mob gathered inside like a receiving committee, her heart sank. Her only comfort was that she'd dressed appropriately. The women all wore floor-length skirts or evening slacks and tops in lustrous fabrics, and the men, suits and ties.

The grand entrance hall where they waited comprised a vast space with a high curved ceiling supported by massive beams, very much in the style she'd come to recognize as typical of Sardinia. The floor was slate-gray, the walls white, the refectory table centered beneath a heavy wrought-iron chandelier so severely plain, it could have come from a monastery. Yet what might otherwise have struck her as stark and rather forbidding was softened by a huge colorful flower arrangement in the middle of the table, muted light from alabaster wall sconces, and vivid oil paintings on the walls.

Soon enough, her other worries eased a little, too. From his aristocratic-looking parents to the smallest child, most spoke at least a smattering of English, and even if they hadn't, there was no mistaking the warmth of their smiles and the way they embraced her into their midst.

Immediately Domenico introduced her, Federico Silvaggio d'Avalos, his tall, handsome father, stepped forward and kissed her hand as gallantly as if she were royalty. "We are honored to welcome you into our home, *signorina*."

His mother, Carmela, well into her fifties and still stunningly beautiful, kissed her on both cheeks, exclaimed at how chilled her face was, and promptly ushered her into a large, elegant salon furnished in pale silks and richly inlaid woods. "We're so happy Domenico brought you to meet us, my dear. Come sit by the fire with me, and get to know my large, noisy family."

A flurry of other introductions followed. The pregnant sister who'd been so sympathetic the day Arlene came down with the migraine, joined her on the sofa. "Hello, again, Arlene. I'm Renata, and this is my husband, Vittorio. Not that you're expected to remember everyone's names," she added, with a laugh. "Even we forget who's who, sometimes, there are so many of us."

"That's true." Another sister put in mischievously. "All four of us girls have married and given our parents grandchildren." She paused. "You're not married, though, are you, Arlene?"

"No."

She smiled sunnily. "What a coincidence. Neither is Domenico."

Apart from the black glare he shot her way, and despite all the trappings of wealth and privilege—the women's jewelry, the plush comfort of Persian rugs, damask upholstery as soft as swansdown, and hand-carved wood polished to a satin shine, not to mention the servants hovering unobtrusively in the background—the atmosphere in the room was relaxed and convivial.

Although the older children were more interested in teasing each other than joining in the adult conversation, the younger ones swarmed around Arlene in wide-eyed curiosity. When one of them, a toddler about eighteen months old, stumbled and fell, his grandmother scooped him onto her lap and comforted him, not caring in the least that he drooled down her shot silk blouse.

A grizzled old dog of indeterminate breed dozed by the fire, but no one shooed him away. No irate parent ordered the children to be quiet, or go play in another room. When the noise level grew too loud, the adults simply raised their voices over it.

Long past her initial nervousness, Arlene basked in the scene. She'd crossed the threshold into their home, a stranger, and in no time at all, they'd accepted her unconditionally. They plied her with questions about her life in Canada, and her newly acquired vineyard. Much to his chagrin and to general laughter, they showed her a photograph of Domenico lying naked on a fur rug when he was a baby, and regaled her with amusing accounts of his boyhood exploits.

This, she thought, soaking up every minute, is what a real family is all about.

Dinner lasted a full three hours, a magnificent feast of traditional Sardinian dishes. *Burrida*, a spicy fish soup, followed by delicately poached sea bream, both served with ice-cold Vermentino bearing the Silvaggio d'Avalos label. Next, a full-bodied red Cannonau, also from the family winery, for the main course of spit-roasted lamb, artichokes and *malloreddus*, small gnocchi-like pasta. For dessert, deep fried ricotta cakes drenched in honey, washed down with a sparkling Moscato from the Gallura hills. And finally, rich dark coffee and tiny, exquisite chocolates filled with minted lemon cream.

Arlene never could have consumed so huge a meal had it not been for the leisurely pace. As it was, she was able to relax between courses and enjoy her surroundings without appearing overly curious.

The dining room itself was a feast for the eyes. Large and square, with French doors opening to a terrace, it sported a table that easily could seat thirty. The musical ping of fine crystal, the discreet clink of heavy sterling on monogrammed china all added to a setting which might have been best described as majestic were it not for the infant high chairs interspersed at regular intervals among the formal furnishings.

"You have a lovely home," Arlene confided to Domenico's mother, during a lull in the conversation.

"Thank you, *cara*. It's really much too big for

just two people, but my children refuse to let me and their father move to something smaller. They claim this is the only place they can all fit around one table at the same time." She glanced at Renata, and Gemma, Domenico's second youngest sister who was also pregnant. "And since the babies keep coming, I suppose they have a point. Do you have brothers and sisters, Arlene?"

"No. I'm an only child."

Only, and lonely—at least until tonight. But Domenico's family had drawn her so seamlessly into their familial web of affection that, for once, she was not on the outside looking in. For once, she felt as if she belonged, even if it was only for a few hours. Not that they fawned over her or gave the impression that they were putting on a show for her benefit. They simply included her.

So many things touched her as the meal progressed. Insignificant things to most people, probably, but to her they spelled all that had been missing from her own upbringing. Lara's husband Edmondo, for example, who left his own food to grow cold while he patiently coaxed his six-year-old son Sebastiano into trying the slivers of lamb he'd been served.

...I didn't say you had to like it, Arlene. I said you had to eat it, and you'll sit there until you do...

Or Domenico's father reaching across the table

to clasp his wife's hand, proof that marriage didn't have to spell the end of love between a man and a woman.

And perhaps most moving of all, Domenico lifting a suddenly fractious niece from her booster seat and cradling her against his shoulder until she fell asleep with her thumb popped firmly in her sweet little rosebud mouth—a sight so unbearably beautiful, so overflowing with affection, that it brought tears to Arlene's eyes.

It was as they all lingered over coffee that the subject arose of a viticulture convention in Paris. "This coming weekend, isn't it?" Renata asked, of no one in particular.

Her uncle Bruno nodded. "That's right. Three days, starting on Friday.

A lively discussion followed, covering speakers, vintners, manufacturers, suppliers and anything else remotely connected to the business of turning grapes into wine.

"You're presenting this year, as usual, Domenico?" his brother-in-law Ignazio inquired.

He nodded, careful not to disturb his sleeping niece. "Once only, on Friday."

Michele, the second eldest sister and the quietest, looked up from wiping honey off her seven-year-old daughter's chin. "You should take Arlene with you. It would be an invaluable experience for her."

"I'm afraid that's out of the question," Arlene said quickly, not about to wait for Domenico to shoot down the idea. If there'd been one flaw in an otherwise perfect evening, it was that he'd remained distinctly aloof from her, as if wanting to make it clear, both to her and his family, that they weren't a couple. Not that he'd totally ignored her. It would have been better if he had. Instead he'd watched her, his blue eyes as sharp and clinical as a surgeon's scalpel. "I'm flying home on Saturday."

"Registration's closed now, anyway," he said.

"Not to you," Lara argued. "Never that. You could show up with twenty extra attendees at the last minute, and they'd be accommodated." She turned to Arlene. "That's the kind of clout our brother wields in vintner circles. They practically kiss his feet when he shows up, he brings such cachet to the occasion."

Fortunately the conversation swung to the pleasures of Paris in October, and soon after, the party came to an end. First the grandchildren were rounded up and bundled into cars by their parents for the short ride home, then it was Arlene's turn to take her leave.

"Come and see us again before you go home," Domenico's mother said kindly, again kissing her on both cheeks.

"Most certainly," his father added. "Don't wait for an invitation. Our door is always open."

"Thank you," she managed, swallowing another sudden clutch of tears, because she knew she wouldn't be coming back. As he had so often throughout the evening, Domenico was again watching her, as if waiting for her to put a foot wrong when she said her goodbyes.

Why? Had she shamed him, in her black skirt and white blouse, with not a single jewel but her pearl earrings to redeem their plainness? Had he decided she wasn't quite good enough to associate with his family? Not sophisticated enough? Or had his aim always been to show her that she didn't fit into his life, and never would?

There was only one way to find out. "Okay, Domenico," she said, the moment they were on the road. "You don't have to pretend any longer. It's nobody but just the two of us now, so 'fess up. What's the real reason you took me to meet your family tonight?"

CHAPTER FIVE

COVERING up his jolt of surprise at the question, Domenico said, "Have you forgotten we already dealt with that subject, Arlene?"

"Remind me again. I'm not sure I remember it accurately."

"I thought it would be an enjoyable experience for everyone involved."

"Including you?"

"Of course including me."

"Then please explain why you spent the entire evening staying as far away from me as possible. Did you have a change of heart once we arrived, and decide you'd made a mistake in inviting me, after all?"

"No."

"I don't believe you. I think you were afraid I'd embarrass you—or worse yet, you hoped I'd embarrass myself."

Inhaling sharply, he slammed on the brakes,

brought the car to a skidding stop on the gravel shoulder at the side of the road and turned to face her. Expert though he was at keeping a poker face, even he couldn't hide his shock. "How the devil could you have done that?"

She shifted in her seat, a slight movement only, but enough for the rustle of silky underthings to whisper alluringly over her skin. "Oh, I don't know," she said, giving another of her elegant little shrugs. "Tucked my napkin in the top of my blouse, and not known which fork to use, perhaps. Or knocked back too much wine and slid under the table in a drunken stupor before the main course was served."

Her reply shook him to the core. Never in his life had he lifted his hand to a woman, but assaulted by so many conflicting emotions he couldn't begin to sort, let alone control, he actually grabbed her by the shoulders and shook her. Not hard, to be sure, and in frustration rather than anger. Nevertheless, her lovely gray eyes turned glassy with unshed tears, and her sweet, vulnerable mouth dropped open in shock.

His mind grew dark. Black and empty as a cave buried deep below the earth's surface. Search though he might, he could find no words to justify his behavior, no lodestar to restore him to himself. Never more at a loss than he was at that moment, he gave up trying to excuse the inexcusable, and once again submitted to the instinct which had driven him for days. He hauled her into his arms and crushed her mouth beneath his.

At first, she resisted, holding herself stiff as a board. Desperate to soften the blow he'd dealt her, he cajoled her by cupping the back of her head in one hand and stroking the other up her throat to caress her jaw.

A tear slipped free. Slid pearl-like down the heated curve of her cheek. He trapped it with his tongue and, finally, the right words, the *only* words that mattered, spilled from him. "I could never be ashamed of you," he whispered into her mouth. "You are the finest thing that ever happened to me. If I stayed away from you, it was because I was afraid to stand too close."

"Why?" Once again, her favorite question emerged, this time uttered on a sigh.

He answered by deepening the kiss, with no thought of pulling away, or of letting matters end there. The hunger he'd tried so hard to contain rampaged through his blood, sending coherent thought tumbling into obscurity. At that moment, he was a man driven beyond reason.

She melted in his embrace. Leaned into him and let her head fall back in utter surrender. The scent of her skin filled him. Drove him beyond the bounds of sophisticated seduction that had always been his trademark.

He knew that stretch of the coast like the back of his hand. Knew that, a few meters ahead, a rough track led into the shelter of the pine trees lining the side of the road. With one arm looped around her shoulder, he left-handedly shifted the roadster into gear, steered it under the dark canopy of branches and killed both engine and headlights.

Stripped of moon and stars by the foliage, night closed around the vehicle, veiling it in cool secrecy. Inside, though, a fire raged, fusing desire into a mass of molten passion as primitive and un-planned as it was unstoppable.

He put his hands on her. Shaped her through the fine lace of her blouse. He found the buttons. Undid them. Pushed aside the silky camisole she wore underneath, to discover the silkier perfection of her breasts.

Her flesh surged against his palm and she let out a tiny gasp of pleasure. It drove him to further madness. Lowering his head, he captured her nipple in his mouth and ran his hand the length of her slender body to her ankles.

Her narrow skirt resisted his intrusion but he, consumed by raging desire, would not be stopped. The sound of a seam splitting made little impres-sion compared to the thundering of his heart.

Her legs were bare and smooth as cream. Freed from the demure confinement imposed by her skirt, they fell slackly apart and turned his invasion into an invitation. The breath seized in his throat at her damp softness; at the warm, sleek privacy to which she gave him access. Already hard, he felt himself pulsing against the fabric of his trousers. Teetering so close to the brink of destruction that he gave no thought to dignity or decency.

An owl swooping suddenly out of the night to brush the tip of one pale wing close to the windshield, saved him from himself. Restored to belated sanity, and appalled at his lack of control, Domenico smoothed her clothing into place and, awash in self-disgust, flung himself away, his chest heaving.

In all the years since he'd lost his virginity at fourteen to a woman twice his age, he'd never once sunk to the level of a backseat Casanova. That in this case there was no backseat and he'd had to make do with two front seats separated by the gearshift console, was a moot point. The fact was, Arlene deserved better than to be subjected to the kind of impatient fumbling that had left her with a torn skirt and a level of sexual frustration that probably matched his own. She deserved a little respect—and a very large apology.

"I am sorry," he said. Then, knowing he owed

her more than that, added, "Not for finding you irresistible, but for showing it so clumsily, and for every other mistake I've made where you're concerned."

"What kind of mistakes?" she whispered into the darkness.

"Letting my pride dictate my actions. That first day, when you mentioned having to meet up with a friend, I jumped to the assumption that you were here with a man." He laughed grimly. "I was eaten up with jealousy."

"I'd never have guessed."

"No," he said. "I'm good at hiding my thoughts and feelings. But the truth is, I wanted to punish you, and I did. The next day, I endangered your health by allowing you to work yourself into a state of complete exhaustion. Your migraine attack was my fault."

She found his face in the darkness and touched his cheek tenderly. "Even you can't take credit for that, Domenico. I should have had enough sense to quit before things came to such a pass. I chose not to, and suffered the consequences."

"I knew better, and should have been more vigilant."

"You've been nothing but helpful and kind and wonderful to me."

He caught her fingers and kissed them. "I'm a

proud, stubborn man, Arlene. I go after what I want with single-minded determination. Don't fool yourself into believing otherwise."

She let her hand trail lightly down his chest. "Do you want me?"

"Yes, I want you," he said, halfway between a laugh and a groan.

"Then take me."

Sorely tempted, he let a beat of silence pass before answering. "Not here. Not now."

"Then when?"

He paused again, weighing the options. He could take her back to his place. They'd be completely alone. It was an unwritten rule among his family that each respected the other's privacy and never showed up on the doorstep without invitation. But there was always the risk of her being seen in the car, and he wasn't ready for the speculation that would arouse.

He could take her to a hotel. But that smacked too much of a cheap one-night stand, and he'd decided years ago he'd never stoop to such lowlife measures. Which left him with what was probably the best and wisest course, and that was to do nothing at all, and so spare them both the pain of having to sever the strands of involvement when it came time for her to leave the island.

Do it, his conscience prompted. *Let her down gently, and walk away before you break her heart.* "You could come with me to Paris," he heard himself suggest.

"I can't afford it," she said.

"I can."

He felt her withdrawal as acutely as if a cold wind had infiltrated the car. "I won't take your money."

"You won't have to. I'll be traveling by private jet. It will cost me no more to add an extra passenger than it will to include an extra guest in my hotel suite."

"Even so, what about Gail? I can't just abandon her."

He heard the longing in her voice. Seduced by it, he said, "She'll meet you in Paris on Sunday morning and you'll fly home together from there."

"Our tickets are for Saturday and don't include a stopover in Paris. We came here via Rome."

"Tickets can be changed, *cara,*" he said, firing up the car and backing it onto the road. "In fact, you can achieve just about anything, if you want it badly enough."

The glow from the illuminated dials on the dash showed her lips pressed together in a way he'd come to recognize meant she was giving serious thought to the idea. "I don't know about that," she finally said. "But I do know I want you."

* * *

At the time, Arlene had been very certain that she knew exactly what she wanted, and also what she'd be getting: one glorious weekend with Domenico Silvaggio d'Avalos, the most exciting man she'd ever known. Not that he'd said it in so many words, but even she wasn't naive enough to think he was promising anything beyond that.

But when he learned she'd never been to Paris, he changed their plans and suggested they leave Sardinia on the Wednesday so that he'd have time to show her something of the city before the convention began. The prospect of four whole days and nights with him left her giddy with anticipation, and if the sensible voice of caution warned her she was getting in over her head, she hushed it. She'd broken the cautious, sensible mold, the day she'd decided to accept her inheritance.

She didn't see him again until the morning of their departure. "After Paris, I'm heading to Chile for a couple of weeks, which means I'll be tied up for the next few days, making sure everything's running smoothly on the homefront before I leave," he told her, when he returned her to her hotel on the Saturday night.

"I understand," she said, steadfastly ignoring his not-too-subtle reminder that, after the coming weekend, they'd be going their separate ways.

"As it happens, I've got a few things to take care of, myself."

Placing his hand in the small of her back, he walked her through the hotel lobby in such a way as to shield her torn skirt from the night clerk's inquisitive stare. "Then it's arranged. I'll have your friend's new flight information delivered tomorrow, and pick you up here at eight on Wednesday morning. We'll be in Paris in time for lunch."

"Sounds wonderful."

As the elevator door whispered open, he dropped a swift, hard kiss on her mouth. "Until Wednesday, then."

Euphoria carried her through the next three days. By Tuesday, she'd refurbished her wardrobe with clothes more suited to private jets and October in Paris, than the beaches of Sardinia. Returning to the millionaire's playground of Alghero, she and Gail scoured the town and found a couple of consignment boutiques stocked with designer fashions in her size. But that they cost her only a fraction of their true value didn't change the fact that she spent more on clothing in two days than she had in the previous two years.

"Think of it as an investment in your future," Gail counseled, when she fretted about the balance owing on her credit card. "This is, after all, as much a business trip as a naughty weekend. You could make some very valuable contacts at the convention, and it's important you project a suitably professional image."

"To the tune of hundreds of dollars?"

"Well, you know what they say. If you want to make an omelet, you have to break a few eggs."

The trouble was, enough clothes to make a four-day, four-night splash in Paris added up to a lot more than just a few eggs. One smart cranberry-red suit, two silk blouses, a pair of tailored slacks, a cashmere sweater, reversible wool cape and basic black velvet dinner dress, plus the two pairs of shoes and ankle-high black suede boots she toted back to the hotel, called for an entire poultry farm!

And that was before she succumbed to the temptation of a misty-mauve, long silk-knit dress and a sinfully gorgeous evening gown shimmering with celadon beading—"because," as Gail reminded her when she hesitated about buying it, "even run-of-the-mill conventions always wind up with a banquet of some sort on the Saturday night, and there's nothing run-of-the-mill about your man and the company he keeps."

Surveying the contents of her suitcase on the Tuesday evening—the "gently used" designer items, supplemented by Gail's silver pumps, matching clutch bag and fake purple pashmina shawl—the full impact of what Arlene had let herself in for finally hit home. She was risking financial and emotional bankruptcy—and for what? A no-promises tryst with a man who hadn't even bothered to pick up the phone and call her since Saturday. A man so dangerously attractive that she was practically guaranteed a broken heart at the end of it all. What use would her fancy new clothes be to her, then?

"I'm a nobody trying to keep up with a very big somebody," she wailed.

"You're an idiot," Gail said bracingly. "Mr. Wonderful puts his pants on one leg at a time, just like any other guy."

But Domenico wasn't at all like any other guy, and the truth of that was driven home with a vengeance, the second he escorted Arlene on board his sleek Gulfstream jet, early on Wednesday morning. The spacious cabin, with its wide aisle, ample headroom, thick carpet and leather seating arrangement spelled the ultimate in luxury and comfort.

She had been too wound up to eat anything before leaving the hotel, but the scant two hours it took to fly from the airport in Olbia to Le Bourget in Paris allowed enough time for a steward to serve them a light breakfast of chilled champagne and orange juice, warm, delicious rolls, fresh fruit and wonderful rich Italian coffee.

"To Paris!" Domenico said, raising his glass

in a toast as the shoreline of Sardinia receded below them.

She nodded, not quite believing she was sitting across from him, a fine, monogrammed serviette on her lap, and a mimosa in a crystal flute clutched nervously between her fingers. Her previous flying experience had been all about paper napkins, packaged snacks and plain orange juice from a disposable plastic glass. But then, she'd never before agreed to what Gail had gleefully described as "a business weekend spiked with sweaty, delicious passion between the sheets, with the sexiest guy to walk the earth since Sean Connery strode around as James Bond."

Sexy, yes, but observant, too, and watching her, Domenico said, "You're very pensive, Arlene. Is something wrong?"

In a word, yes! A sleepless night had merely intensified her doubts. Plain, ordinary Arlene Russell didn't belong in a private jet with a man like him. "I'm rather overwhelmed, I guess. I've never been whisked away to one of the great capitals of Europe by someone I've only just met."

"If you're having second thoughts about coming away with me, rest assured I'll not pressure you into doing anything you're not ready for. You will set the pace of our time together, *cara*, not I."

"That's hardly the agreement we made last Saturday. I'm not about to repay your generosity by…" She stopped, unable to put into words what they both knew she meant.

He suffered no such qualms. "By not sleeping with me? Arlene, please! Just because I find you desirable doesn't mean you owe me sexual favors. Over the next few days, you'll meet some of the foremost viticulturists in the world. I'll consider myself well rewarded if you make the most of that opportunity." He shrugged then, and smiled. "And if we happen also to make love? Well, that will be a bonus."

Avoiding his gaze, she stroked her hand over the butter-soft leather arm of her seat. "I wondered if perhaps you'd changed your mind about that. We haven't spoken since Saturday, and when you picked me up this morning, you were very…businesslike."

"You mean, I didn't kiss you?"

He was altogether too good at divining her thoughts. Flushing, she said, "Not even on the cheek."

"Is that what's left you so much at odds?" He laughed, and leaning across the table, caught her chin and brought his mouth to hers. "You taste delectable," he murmured, when at last he drew away again. "And if you think I've kept my distance because I've had a change of heart, you couldn't be more mistaken."

Her mood lifted at that, and she found it easier to focus on the here and now, and leave the future to take care of itself. If this magical few days was to mark the grand finale of her experience with this incredible man, she wouldn't let her insecurities cloud it. Twenty years from now, she wanted the details etched so clearly in her memory that it seemed they had happened just yesterday.

As the jet began its descent over Paris, Domenico pointed out famous landmarks she'd only ever read about, or seen on television or in the movies. Her face pressed to the window, she caught her first glimpse of the Eiffel Tower, the Arc de Triomphe, the bridges across the Seine, Notre Dame, Sacré-Coeur. The names and images unfolded below, gilded with autumn sunlight and the romantic ambience which had defined the city for centuries.

When they emerged from the airport, a chauffeur-driven Mercedes waited to take them to their hotel. Arlene hoped it would be modest enough that her beleaguered credit card could cover the cost of staying there, because she had no intention of letting Domenico pay. It was enough that he'd taken care of their travel arrangements and used his influence to get her registered at the convention.

She realized how fruitless her hopes were when the car drew to a stop and she found herself standing before the legendary Paris Ritz. Even she knew it was among the most expensive and luxurious hotels in the world. Frozen with dismay, she clutched Domenico's arm and skidded to a stop. "The convention's being held *here?*"

"I never stay in the convention hotel, *cara*," he said, calmly propelling her inside the beautiful eighteenth-century building. "Too crowded, too noisy and not nearly enough privacy."

"But I can't afford this place!"

"I can."

"That's not the point!"

"Then what is?"

"That I have my pride. I've gone along with everything else you've suggested, but I refuse to let you pay for my accommodation."

He glanced meaningfully at the people milling around the ornate lobby. "We will not discuss the matter here, Arlene. It can wait until we are alone."

But that didn't happen until she found herself in a suite of rooms overlooking the Vendôme Gardens, and the sheer magnificence of the setting alone was enough to render her speechless. Elegant antique furniture, priceless *objets d'art*, paintings, Persian rugs, huge floral arrangements—try as she might, taking it all in was impossible. Simply put, she had never in her life *seen* anything so exquisite, let alone found herself immersed in it.

Stunned, she turned to Domenico. "What am I doing in this place?"

"This," he said, and kissed her for the second time that day; a long, achingly beautiful kiss.

She struggled to keep her head, to stand by her principles. But however magnificent the Ritz, it couldn't hold a candle to Domenico Silvaggio d'Avalos when he set out to seduce. She could walk away from the trappings of the rich and famous, and never know a moment's regret. She could not walk away from him.

Not that she didn't try. Tearing her mouth free, she whispered, "I don't belong here, Domenico."

"Then leave," he said, holding her tighter. Trapping her in his magnetic aura.

"You don't understand...!"

"What don't I understand, Arlene?" he murmured, drawing out her name on a long breath, and turning it into an endearment.

"I'm afraid. Out of my element. I don't know where all this is leading."

"Then we'll be afraid together, because I don't know that, either."

She sighed, her gaze locked helplessly with his.

"I don't believe you know the meaning of fear. You're invincible."

He shook his head. "I'm just a man, *tesoro*," he said quietly, stroking her face. "Because I happen to have more money than some doesn't make me better or worse than they are. It doesn't define who I am. Leave if you must, but do it because you don't wish to stay with me, not because of my wealth, and not because you're afraid I'm trying to buy you. I have a standing reservation on this particular suite, and as I believe I told you last Saturday, the price remains the same regardless of how many guests occupy it. And if it matters at all, there are two bedrooms. I'll be sleeping in mine until, or unless, you invite me to share yours."

How could she leave, after that? How could she turn away from his candid blue gaze, or doubt his decency, his integrity?

Sensing he'd won her over, he led her by the hand to the tall salon windows overlooking the gardens. "Let's not waste any more time standing here arguing over trivialities, not when the sun's shining, and all Paris waits to meet you." He fingered her light sweater, which had been more than adequate for Sardinia's weather. "Put on something warmer, and I'll introduce you to one of my favorite cities."

* * *

They began with a trip on a *bateau-mouche*, one of a fleet of long tour boats that plied the waters of the Seine. As the vessel glided by the Ile de la Cité and the Ile Saint-Louis, she sat beside Domenico on the glass-covered deck and breathed in the history of the dazzling monuments.

The names of the people who'd immortalized the ancient city branded themselves on her brain. Marie Antoinette… Victor Hugo… Charles Dickens…Toulouse-Lautrec… The list was endless, fascinating.

The wind had picked up and turned the morning chilly when at last they disembarked on the Left Bank. Copper leaves from the chestnut trees swirled around her ankles as Domenico hurried her along the street to a tiny riverside bistro, and she was glad she'd changed into the slim-fitting black slacks and scarlet turtleneck sweater. With her cape thrown over her shoulders and her feet snug in their suede boots, she almost felt as if she belonged in chic, elegant Paris.

"So how did you enjoy the *bateau-mouche*?" he wanted to know, after they'd been shown to a table next to a blue and white enameled woodstove, and were enjoying a glass of red wine, which the waiter poured from a carafe on the counter dividing the kitchen from the eating area.

"Amazing! The most breathtaking experience

of my life! If I didn't see anything else, I'd go home satisfied with what I saw this morning."

"Oh, that was just the aperitif, Arlene," he promised, the heat in his eyes rivaling that thrown out by the logs in the stove. "The best is yet to come. Now tell me what you'd like for lunch."

"You decide," she said, so exhilarated that she wondered why she'd ever entertained a moment's hesitation about being with him. "I'm happy to leave myself in your hands."

After scrutinizing the chalkboard listing the day's offerings, he chose oyster stew, a rich, steaming dish served in individual casserole dishes, accompanied by a baguette fresh from the *boulangerie* next door, and a dish of unsalted butter.

"What do you think of the wine?" he asked at one point.

"Nice legs!" she replied mischievously, and just like that set a lighthearted tone she'd not often experienced with him before then.

As a result, their simple lunch in that unpretentious little bistro marked a shift in their relationship. They laughed and talked as easily as if they'd known each other for months instead of days.

The sexual tension remained, of course. She knew that, for her, it always would. It was as much a part of her as breathing. But for the first time since they'd met, she relaxed enough to stop worrying about what he might be thinking of her, or how he might be feeling about her, and simply had fun with him.

He sensed the change in her. "Still feeling overwhelmed?" he asked, trapping her hand in his, as they lingered over the last of their wine.

Knowing he was referring to her comments during the flight, she shook her head, her heart so full, so grateful, that for a moment she couldn't speak.

"No more doubts or fears that you've let yourself in for more than you bargained for?"

"None," she managed, over the lump in her throat.

"I'm glad," he said. "I want to see you smile more often, hear you laugh the way you have this last hour, as if there's no place you'd rather be than here, with me."

"There isn't," she admitted. "We haven't known one another very long, but you've become very...important to me."

Important? The inadequacy of the word made her shudder. He'd become crucial to her very existence! He filled all the empty corners of her heart. She was captivated by him. Had been almost from the moment she first set eyes on him.

"How long we've known each other isn't an issue," he murmured, his gaze seeming to devour her. "What counts is not settling for the safe and ordinary, but being brave enough to recognize and hold on to the remarkable whenever it happens to come along, and despite the risks it might entail." He stopped and tilted his head to one side, his brows lifted in inquiry. "You're smiling again. Why?"

"Because you struck a chord with your remark about settling for the safe and ordinary," she said. "Until recently, that's what I feel I've always done."

"How so?"

She hesitated a moment. Sharing her past didn't come easily. But he squeezed her hand and said quietly, "Tell me, Arlene. I'll understand."

"All right." Quickly, before she lost her nerve, she plunged in. "You know about my parents' divorce and how I never really got to spend any time with my father."

"Yes," he said. "You lost him when you were very young, and from what you told me, it doesn't seem your mother was able to fill the hole his death left in your life."

"It wasn't that she couldn't, Domenico, it was that she wouldn't. The only reason she fought my father for custody was that she knew he wanted me. She remarried when I was eleven, and decided that she didn't want to be saddled with a child anymore. I spent the next seven years trying to prove I deserved her love but eventually had to settle for her tolerating me, instead. The day I graduated with honors from high school, she informed me that, at eighteen, I should be living in my own place, and kicked me out of the house. I'd hoped to become a lawyer, but I couldn't support myself and afford law school as well, so I settled for becoming a legal secretary."

She stopped rather abruptly then. Adding the rest—that she'd turn thirty in February, that her biological clock deafened her with its frantic ticking and she longed to have a baby, but that until she met him, she'd resigned herself to remaining single because she hadn't met a man she could love with her whole heart—was best kept to herself. Domenico didn't strike her as a man given to panic, but her baring her soul that far would surely send him running out the door in a cold sweat. It was enough that she'd already confided to him things she'd previously shared only with Gail.

"Such a woman," he stated unequivocally in the pause that followed, "is a poor excuse for a mother."

Arlene shrugged. "I came to terms with who my mother is, years ago. I can't change her. The only thing I have control over is my own destiny."

"That's all any of us can do," he observed.

"Yes, but it took inheriting my great-uncle's vineyard for me to realize that. The challenges in my new life—and yes, the risks, too—have shaken me out of my comfort zone and made me realize I was suffocating on the safe and dull and merely tolerable. I want to *live*, not simply exist. I want to know the thrill of accomplishment, even if it's sometimes flavored with setbacks. I'm not saying I think I should always have the best, or be the best, because that's not how life plays out. But I'll do without before I'll settle for second best again."

"Which is exactly as it should be." He wove her fingers more tightly in his. "Thank you for trusting me enough to share what I know are painful memories. They give me greater understanding into what makes you the woman you are today."

She laughed rather uncertainly. "Oh dear! I thought men preferred women with a little mystery to them."

"A little, perhaps, but you've whet my appetite. I very much want to learn more about you, Arlene."

"Well, not right now, if you don't mind," she said lightly. "Not with Paris waiting to be explored."

Rising, he pulled her to her feet and draped her cape snugly around her shoulders. "Then let's get on with it, *cara mia*. How would you most like to spend the rest of the afternoon?"

"Visiting Notre Dame," she replied, without a moment's hesitation. Ever since she was a girl and had read Victor Hugo's classic novel of the tragic hunchback, Quasimodo, she'd dreamed of climbing the towers, and looking out over the rooftops of Paris.

"Then Notre Dame it will be," he said, and led her to the street again.

The reality of the cathedral, its majesty and atmosphere, so far exceeded her expectations that she couldn't imagine anything else the day had to offer could match it. Until, with dusk fast approaching, she and Domenico returned to the Ritz, and she found herself preparing for the evening ahead—and the night that would follow.

CHAPTER SIX

HE COULD see in her face, and the way she moved—gingerly, as if everything hurt—that the grueling climb up and down the towers, coupled with a very long day, had exhausted her. Not that she'd been willing to admit it.

"Of course it wasn't too much for me," she'd insisted gamely, after it was over and she'd gazed her fill at the Paris skyline, her expression filled with a wonder that was almost childlike in its purity. "I wouldn't have missed it for the world."

She had stamina, he'd grant her that. And it looked as if she was going to need it. From everything she'd told him and what he'd gathered from his contacts in the area, she'd inherited not the bucolic paradise she envisioned, but a disaster that could ruin her. The so-called "help" she thought he'd given amounted to nothing compared to what she'd need when she finally confronted the difficulties facing her.

He couldn't protect her from that, but he could see to it that these few days in Paris were as idyllic as his considerable power and money could make them. She'd need a few perfect memories to sustain her, once she was flung into the arduous and unforgiving business of viticulture. Right at that moment, however, she was fading visibly.

"I couldn't get a dinner reservation before nine," he told her, which was a lie. Regardless of the hour, there was always a table for him at Clarice's, the elegant little restaurant he often patronized, as much for its exceptional cuisine as its convenient location to the hotel. "We've got nearly three hours before we have to leave, and I suggest you use some of that time to relax."

"I think I will." She flexed one knee and winced. "In fact, I think I'll soak in a nice, hot bath."

"Excellent idea," he said, sternly turning his thoughts away from the image of her long, lovely body in all its naked glory.

He waited until she'd shut herself in her room before attending to the calls waiting to be answered, as indicated by the flashing light on the telephone. Ten in all, nine of which he returned, and one he ignored. That Ortensia Costanza was also in Paris for the convention didn't surprise him, but he had no intention of allowing her to interfere with his time there.

Unbuttoning his shirt, he ambled to his own bathroom, shed the rest of his clothes and stepped into the shower. Jets of hot water pummeled his body, sluicing away the dust of the day, and dulling the edge of weariness travel always induced. Drying off, he shaved, combed his hair and helped himself to the bathrobe the hotel supplied.

Left to his own devices, he'd have ordered a meal delivered to the suite and watched something mindless on television, an indulgence he seldom allowed himself in the normal order of things. He suspected that, had he asked, Arlene might have gone along with the idea, but lounging around in a state of semiundress was a temptation he wasn't about to fool himself into believing he could withstand.

On the other hand, he wasn't a complete barbarian, and the bottle of Krug he'd had sent up wouldn't remain at optimum temperature indefinitely. Confident she'd still be relaxing in the bath, he collected the wine and two glasses, and let himself into her bedroom. "Are you decent in there, Arlene?" he said, tapping on her bathroom door.

She let out a muffled yelp of surprise. "Of course I'm not decent! I'm in the tub!"

"Hidden under a blanket of bubbles, I'm sure."

"Well…yes."

"Good enough." Not waiting for permission, he pushed open the door and strolled to where she reclined in the marble tub with only her head visible above a snowy mound of froth. She'd turned off the bank of lights above the vanity and left the room swathed in the flickering shadows of lavender-scented candles.

Sputtering, she regarded him from wide gray eyes. Steam curled around her face and left tendrils of hair clinging damply to her forehead. "What do you think you're doing?"

"It's customary to enjoy a little champagne when bathing at leisure at the Paris Ritz," he said blandly, pouring the wine and offering her a glass.

One slender arm emerged from the bubbles, a modest amount of body, to be sure, but enough for his first inkling that perhaps he'd underestimated his powers of resistance. He cleared his throat and backed to the vanity, a safe distance away. "*Salute*—or, as they say in France, *à la vôtre!*"

"I don't believe this," she muttered, eyeing him mistrustfully.

"Then simply enjoy it, *cara*. And stop looking so fearful. I promise I haven't laced the wine with an aphrodisiac. You're not going to lose your inhibitions and leap all over me."

Her gaze remaining fused with his, she took a

tentative sip. "Is this how you treat all the women you entertain here? Catching them at a disadvantage, and plying them with alcohol?"

"The only women I've entertained here are my sisters. Fond of them though I am, serving them champagne in the bathtub doesn't fall under the heading of brotherly obligation. They have husbands to take care of things like that. You, however, have only me."

"Is that how you view me? As an obligation?"

"You know very well that I do not. I've made no secret of how very attractive I find you, and how much I desire you. Not even you, Arlene, can mistake that for obligation."

She swallowed and concentrated very hard on the bubbles rising in her glass. "You must find me laughably unsophisticated that I'd agree to come away with you for the weekend, yet be so self-conscious about your seeing me naked."

"But that's the whole point, Arlene," he said gently. "I see only as much of you as you care to show me, and I can say in all honesty that, at this moment, it amounts to very little."

But enough for his imagination to complete the picture and send the blood surging to his loins. Glad of the dim light, he adjusted the layer of thick terry cloth covering him and willed his nether regions to behave. A pointless exercise, of course. A man's greatest weakness was his inability to control or disguise his arousal.

Fortunately she was too concerned with maintaining her own modesty to worry about his. "This place we're going for dinner," she said, running her finger over the rim of her glass, "is it very dressy?"

"It's not black tie, if that's what you mean, but yes, I'd say it's moderately dressy. Does that present a problem for you?"

Her suds-draped shoulder peeped out of the bubbles in a brief shrug. "Not really. I just don't want to embarrass you."

They'd had this conversation once already, just last Saturday, and he thought he'd made it plain enough then that nothing she said or did could ever embarrass him. Yet looking at her now, he saw an abyss of uncertainty in her eyes, and he knew exactly its cause. "Do yourself a favor, Arlene, and forget everything your mother taught you," he said, a flash of anger at the woman's willful destruction of her only daughter's confidence taking him by surprise.

She stifled a laugh. "That's unusual advice. I'm sure neither you nor your sisters follow it."

"My sisters and I are blessed with a mother who has our best interests at heart. It would appear the same can't be said about yours, and I venture to guess the reason is that she's jealous of you."

"Oh, hardly! My mother is the epitome of chic. I'm a terrible disappointment to her."

"In what way?"

She wrinkled her elegant little nose. "I'm plain."

"That," he said flatly, "is a matter of opinion. Of greater interest, at least to me, is what makes her so unfeeling. Can you imagine telling a child of yours she was plain, even if you believed it to be true?"

"Never!" Her eyes blazed with fierce intensity and she sat up slightly out of the water so that it lapped in soapy little waves against the top of her breasts. "If I had a daughter...*oh, if I had a daughter...!* I would tell her every day how beautiful she was—or him, if I had a son—and it would be true because, in my eyes, they would be beautiful! The most precious, beautiful children in the entire world!"

Realizing too late that he'd struck a nerve, he stared at her, taken aback by her impassioned response. "You crave a child," he said.

She shrank up to her chin under the drift of foaming bubbles, as if trying to hide her most shameful secret. "I'd like to have a baby, yes."

"What's stopping you?"

"A husband, for a start. I'm surprised you'd even ask, given your views on marriage and families."

"Are you saying you've never met a man you'd even consider marrying?"

Her lashes fluttered down, lustrous gold-tipped veils shielding her eyes. "You ask too many questions, Domenico, and this water's growing cold."

And he was treading on dangerous territory. Marriage and children were topics he avoided discussing with women, lest they leap to unwarranted conclusions about his intentions.

Glancing at his watch, he said smoothly, "It's time you finished getting ready, anyway. We've got only about forty-five minutes before we have to leave."

The breath of relief she let out as the door closed behind him sent a drift of foam sailing over the side of the tub to the marble floor. The water might have grown cool, but her blood raced fast and hot through her veins.

She'd almost had a heart attack when he showed up without so much as a by-your-leave. Not because he might have caught her naked as the day she was born, but because he'd surprised her in a fantasy woven around him that had left her nipples hard as pebbles and the secret flesh between her thighs tingling.

She wasn't a virgin. Afraid she might be missing something spectacular, she'd succumbed to the pleadings of a man she'd dated when she was twenty-two. They'd "done it" in his bed, in his apartment. He'd said all the right things, and been very proud of his performance. And left her wishing she'd stayed home with a good book. The best she could say about the experience had been that it was over quickly. She had no idea how it felt to climax.

She'd decided then that sex was vastly over-rated and highly undignified, and no one she'd met since had persuaded her to think differently. Until she met Domenico, and with him….

She pressed her hands to her flaming cheeks, mortified. She'd taken shimmering pleasure in letting him touch her intimately. Had known a coiling tension that left the skin behind her knees dotted with goose bumps. A quiver had spread from the pit of her stomach to her womb, leaving her trembling on the brink of discovery. And all this in the front seat of his car.

So much for dignity! Yet she'd felt not a scrap of shame, and not a moment's regret beyond the fact that it all ended much too soon. *I want you,* she'd whispered.

Well, here he was, hers for the taking, and how did she respond? With a pathetically coy show of reluctance that bordered on outright deception. There were names for women who played that kind of game, and she didn't like to think of them being applied to her.

"So start being honest with yourself and with him," she murmured to her flushed image in the bathroom mirror. "If you really do want him, stop dithering and make the first move before you run out of time."

The truth of that stayed with her, prodding her to action all the time she was smoothing body lotion over her limbs and fashioning her hair into a sleek chignon. It whispered to her as she drew a mascara wand over her lashes and slipped into delicate cream silk underwear—she'd always had a weakness for pretty lingerie, as if being glamorous underneath made up for looking so plain on the surface. It nudged her memory as she sifted through the items in her closet.

The night she'd lost her virginity, she'd worn a sweater whose neck fit so tight that it had become stuck over her ears when Whatever-his-name-was had tried to take it off. One of her earrings had flown across the room and she'd stood there, helpless and humiliated, with half her face squished into a shape nature never intended, while he struggled to free the other half.

She wasn't about to suffer a repeat performance again tonight. Too much was at stake. Domenico might consider her untutored in the art of love, but he didn't have to find her ridiculous, as well. Her choice of what to wear would be dictated by how gracefully she could shed it—or he could remove it. Because, one way or another, she would wake up tomorrow morning his mistress, and if her reign had to be short, she would make sure it was also very, very sweet. For both of them.

In the end, she decided on the misty-mauve silk-knit dress. Long but simply styled, it was dressy without being ostentatious, and clung smoothly in all the right places. Gail's purple pashmina shawl, silver pumps and clutch bag, and a pair of her dangling crystal earrings provided the finishing touches.

That she'd chosen well was immediately apparent when she joined Domenico in the salon. "I'll be the envy of every man who sees me with you tonight," he said hoarsely, holding her at arm's length, the better to examine the gown's classic Empire lines. The evening was off to a good start.

Clarice's lived up to every idealized concept Arlene had ever harbored of what an intimate, elegant Parisian restaurant should be. Framed oil paintings, illuminated by discreet spotlights, glowed against burgundy damask wall panels above rich mahogany wainscoting. Winged armchairs, upholstered in faded tapestry, snugged up to round tables covered by thick white linen cloths whose hems swept the carpeted floor. Candlelight glimmered softly on sterling place settings and sparkled on crystal.

A harpist half-hidden behind a lacquered screen filled the room with melody. The white-aproned waiters were discreet, melting into the shadows when they weren't needed, and appearing silently the very second they were.

She and Domenico dined at leisure on artichoke soup with wild thyme, and lobster terrine. On boneless breast of duck artfully arranged on Belgian endive sautéed in butter and sprinkled with slivers of toasted almond. On apricots from Turkey and *crème fraîche* drizzled with vanilla sugar. And with every delectable mouthful, every sip of exquisite vintage wine, she was aware of his compelling gaze reminding her of the deadline she'd set herself.

It was close to midnight when they returned to the Ritz. The witching hour, she thought dizzily, unable to suppress a nervous shiver as he closed the door to their suite and slipped the lock in place. During their absence, someone from housekeeping had replenished the flower arrangements and left crystal brandy snifters and a bottle of cognac on a silver tray.

"A nightcap?" Domenico inquired, and she was tempted to say yes, if only to prolong the moment of unvarnished truth when she revealed how deeply she ached for him.

But drinking herself into oblivion was not her style and would solve nothing. "Thank you, but no. I've had enough for tonight."

"You enjoyed the evening?"

There it was: the perfect opening for her to go up to him, take his hand, look him straight in the eye and say something along the lines of, *It was wonderful, Domenico, but it's not over yet.* "Very much," she said, and faked a yawn behind her hand.

The smile he turned on her made a mockery of her attempt at subterfuge. "You're exhausted."

"Yes. It's been a very long day." An endless day, she thought, finding it hard to believe it was only this morning that she'd woken up in Sardinia. She'd lived a hundred thrilling lifetimes since then—and died a thousand tiny deaths inspired by her chronic fear that she wouldn't measure up to expectation.

He poured an inch of cognac into a snifter. "You should go to bed."

"Yes." Still, she hesitated, mustering her courage. Willing herself to say simply, *I'm ready, Domenico. Please make love to me tonight.* Mutely imploring him with her eyes to help her. To make it easy for her to cross the line and take that final step.

Cradling the brandy balloon between his fingers, he came to her and kissed her. On the cheek. "I'll say good night, then. Sleep well."

She swallowed, the sting of tears so close to betraying her that the best she could manage was a choked, "Thank you," before fleeing the scene.

Coward! she upbraided herself, making her way through her bedroom to the bathroom. But its carrara marble floors and fixtures, its gold plated taps and fittings offered no comfort. They were as alien to her world as the notion that she could boldly seduce a man into her bed.

Idiot! she could almost hear Gail saying. *Stop selling yourself short, and seize the moment. It's not too late.*

But she'd smeared her mascara with tears, and the chignon she'd so carefully constructed was coming undone. As a femme fatale, she left a lot to be desired. Better to sleep on it and see what tomorrow brought.

Glad to have reached a decision she could adhere to, she washed her face, brushed her teeth, and put on her pretty pink nightgown before hanging up her dress in the vast wardrobe. Whoever had replaced the bouquets in the salon had also turned down her bed, she noticed, and left a chocolate and a single red rose on her pillow.

Chocolate and red roses; the food and flowers of lovers. Dark melting sweetness on her tongue, just like his kiss. Petals smooth and cool as velvet flesh brushing against hers...

Suddenly irresolute, she swung her gaze to the door separating her from him. If she were to open it now, and go to him, letting her state of undress speak for itself, would he understand and spare her having to ask? Would he welcome her? Or had she tested his patience too severely?

Only one way to find out! Gail's voice teased across the miles.

Tentatively she turned the knob and eased open the door. Peeped out, and...

And nothing. A small table lamp cast enough light for her to see that the salon was empty and the door to his room closed. The brandy he'd poured remained untouched in its glass.

Relief warred with disappointment. Once again, she'd been spared making a decision. Or so she believed. But he was an invisible magnet, drawing her helplessly closer. Her bare feet sighed over the Persian rug. At her touch, his door swung open.

Outside his open window, the night wind whispering through the branches of the trees in the Vendôme Gardens lured her across the threshold. The moon sailing above the slate rooftops of Paris cast a blue sheen over the big wide bed—and him, half-covered by the top sheet, impervious to her presence.

She approached him stealthily, ready to flee if he stirred.

Except for the steady rise and fall of his chest, he remained immobile. His hair, black as ink, fell across his forehead. His lashes, disgracefully long, sprayed thick and lush above his cheeks. Textured by moonlight, the contoured skin of his shoulders, his arms, revealed underlying muscles honed to sleek perfection.

She touched him. She couldn't help herself. Her hand took on a mind of its own and came to rest lightly against his chest. He was warm, vital.

And awake. *"Ciao,"* he said, his eyes dark gleaming pools in his face.

She let out a gasp. The die was cast. There was no sneaking back to her own room; no pretending she'd wandered into his by accident. "I didn't mean to wake you," she whimpered, and went to snatch back her hand.

His own shot out and captured her wrist, holding her firmly in place "I was not sleeping, Arlene. Far from it," he said, and to prove his point, slid her hand from his chest and over the flat plane of his stomach to the thick, hot ridge of flesh resting against his belly. "I was thinking about you and wondering how long I'd have to wait to possess you."

She almost fainted with fright. In the space of a heartbeat, she'd gone from laying an innocuous hand on his chest, to holding his penis. It throbbed against her palm, silky and determined. Eager and urgent.

What did he want her to do next?

The possible ways she might seduce him had occurred to her. Of course they had. But not once had she envisioned this. Her focus had been on letting him know with a glance, a word, that she was ready to take the next step. With enticing him into her room, then letting him take it from there.

How had she, whose experience in the art of lovemaking was about on a par with a beginner pianist, skipped straight from recognizing the correct sequence of simple notes, to performing a complicated overture she'd never played before?

"Arlene?" His voice swam out of the shadows, as much a caress as a question. *Ar-lay-na*…

"I don't know what to do," she said on a tight breath. "I want so badly to please you but I don't know how."

"You please me immeasurably, simply by being here. As for what happens next, why don't we begin with this?"

Releasing her hand, he drew her down next to him on the bed. He touched her lightly, tracing a path from the inside of her arm to her shoulder. He stroked up the side of her neck to her ear and drew circles around its perimeter with his fingertip.

She closed her eyes, caught in a web of sensation so pleasurably hypnotic, every cell in her body relaxed. His lips mapped a leisurely tour of her face, drifting from her eyelids to her nose; from her cheekbones to her jaw. By the time he settled his mouth on hers, she was trembling. When his tongue nudged the seam of her lips, she accepted him with the desperation of a starving woman.

If this was all he gave her, it would be enough, she thought, almost afraid of the strange, delicious sensations gathering force in the distant corners of her body. But he was less easily satisfied. Trailing his tongue to her ear, he probed deeply.

The effect was devastating and instantaneous. Jolted from passive acceptance, she moaned and clawed at him, digging her nails into the solid bulk of his shoulders. Her insides turned a slow somersault. A sharp, electric spasm clutched between her legs.

Blindly she turned her face and nudged his mouth with hers, craving again the dark penetration of his predatory tongue. Begging to taste him, to be possessed by him.

He curved one arm around her waist and pulled her closer. Her body rolled sweetly against his, discovering the smooth texture of his torso, except for a dusting of hair on his chest, and a denser, silkier swatch arrowing from his navel to his groin. His legs meshed with hers, became tangled in the folds of her nightgown.

He plucked at it. "This has to go, *tesoro*."

It did. Abetting him, the silky fabric slithered willingly away from her body and left her naked before him. After, a moment of pure, still silence hung in the air, eventually broken by his indrawn breath. "You are touched with moonlight," he murmured huskily, "and you are beautiful."

The next moment, his mouth was at her breast, hot and damp, and his hand was skimming past her hips. He touched her, sweeping his finger between her thighs to stroke the cloistered folds of her femininity. With tactile finesse, he induced another spasm, this one so exquisitely acute that she arched off the mattress with a muffled cry.

He soothed her, murmuring something in Italian, something unintelligible yet oddly reassuring, and touched her again, repeatedly. A roaring coursed through her body, building in intensity until, suddenly, the motherboard that was her brain short-circuited into a thousand dazzling sparks.

"Domenico!" she sobbed, urging him past caution with hands grown clever in their desperation. Opening her legs wide, she pulled him on top of her with superhuman strength, and guided him to where her flesh throbbed and ached for his complete possession.

For one glorious instant, his penis pulsed against her, steely silk straining against supple, molten satin. Then, cursing, he flung himself away to sheath himself swiftly, expertly, in a condom. Then, "I'm here," he ground out, turning to face her again. And he was. Above her, around her and most of all, deep inside her. Answering her feverish need with his own. Driving into her in a ritual that was at once more primitive and more refined than anything she'd ever thought to know.

Cupping her bottom in his hands, he lifted her hips and buried himself to the hilt. Instinctively she wrapped her legs around his waist, trapping him. Wanting all of him.

The blood thundered in her veins. Her vision blurred, grew red and hazy. She was dimly aware that his breathing had grown ragged, that his chest heaved as if he wrestled with odds far beyond the scope of mortal man to control.

"Stay with me," he muttered hoarsely, his thrusting rhythm growing frenzied. And to make sure she did, he slid his hand between their bodies and touched her again, just once.

It was enough. She peaked a second time, a long, exquisite explosion that destroyed him and her both. He buried his face at her neck. His body tensed, shuddered, and with a mighty groan that echoed to the farthest reaches of her soul, he climaxed.

Many minutes passed before he moved or spoke. She didn't care. She could have remained all night bearing the weight of his body. Its warmth, the beat of his heart against hers, his breath fanning damply against her skin, they were all she needed to be utterly, completely happy.

Not him, though. When at length he stirred and clicked on the bedside lamp, the searching gaze he turned on her had her reaching to cover herself with the sheet. "What?" she said fearfully. "Shall I go back to my own room?"

He stroked her face tenderly. "Why would you do that, *cara mia*, when so much of the night remains and there is room to spare in my bed?"

"I'm afraid I disappointed you."

"Disappointed?" He rolled the word around on his tongue as if it were a new and rather unpleasant taste.

"Well, you probably guessed I'm not very good at this."

"Perhaps you're not," he said, flinging off the sheet and subjecting her to intense scrutiny. "Perhaps you need more practice. Come here, my darling."

Squirming under his gaze, she begged, "Turn off the light!"

"No," he said. "I want to watch you, the next time I make you come."

And he took her again, this time putting his mouth where before he'd touched her only with his finger, and what would have shocked her yesterday took her to new heights of ecstasy now. The tension built in her until she shattered into a million pieces and thought she'd never find herself again.

"Yes," he said, kissing away the tears rolling down her face and stroking the hair from her brow. "Just so, my lovely."

When he entered her, she closed her eyes, but he would have none of it. "Look at me, Arlene," he commanded. "See for yourself how much you please me."

And he thrust into her faster, more urgently. The sweat gleamed on his skin. His eyes turned midnight-blue. He growled low in his throat, a fierce primeval sound. A man engaged in a battle he couldn't win, yet fighting to his last, desperate breath to tame the hunger bent on destroying him.

His orgasm was a terrifying, beautiful thing beyond description. Watching him, she felt herself drowning in passion. He'd done more than captivate her. He'd stolen her heart forever. She'd fallen hopelessly, helplessly in love with him.

The realization struck like an arrow, so terrifying and glorious that she surged up against him, her eyes wide with shock.

CHAPTER SEVEN

MISUNDERSTANDING, Domenico froze. "Did I hurt you, *tesoro*?"

"No," she was quick to reply.

But she knew he would, if she didn't control her runaway imagination. Falling in love with him wasn't an option. For her, it meant commitment, marriage, children. And within hours of meeting her, he'd made it clear enough how he felt about all that.

I'm waiting for the right woman to come along.

You have a list of requirements she must meet, in order to qualify as your wife, do you?

Of course. Happiness, like sexual compatibility and physical attraction, will run secondary to suitability....

And therein lay the problem. Plain, ordinary Arlene Russell no more measured up as suitable wife material for a man like him, than she belonged in a corporate jet or a plush suite at the

Paris Ritz. From the very beginning of her association with him, she'd been miles out of her depth, socially and economically. To delude herself into believing otherwise, just because they'd had unbelievably fabulous sex, would invite nothing but a badly broken heart.

On the other hand, what was so marvelous about the emotional limbo she'd occupied for so long? Wasn't she the one who'd declared so positively that life without risk, without adventure, sapped the spirit from a person and left her numb? Why else had she consigned her safe, dull existence in Toronto to hell, and chanced everything on a fresh start in a new place?

To backslide now and let fear negate the splendor of the passion she'd shared with Domenico would be a crime. In one respect, at least, he'd elevated her from the ordinary to the sublime with his persuasive finesse.

"Arlene? What is it? What are you thinking?"

Snapping out of her introspection, she looked up and found him watching her. No trace remained of the tempest that had consumed him. His breathing was normal and his eyes, which minutes before had grown dark with passion, were once again a sharply focused, uncompromising blue.

"That I owe you so much more than I can ever

repay," she said. "Until tonight, I had no idea making love could be so incredible."

He lowered his lashes in a long, slow blink. "What are you trying to say, Arlene? That you came to me a virgin?"

"No. But would it have mattered if I did?"

"Only insofar that I'd have tempered my own desire with more consideration for your needs. A woman's first time with a man should be memorable for its tenderness and I..." He shook his head in evident self-disgust. "I was caught up too much in my own pleasure to give proper thought to yours."

She touched a hand to his face. "Don't say that, Domenico. No woman could ask for a better lover—not that I'm exactly experienced in that department, as you probably guessed, but I do know wonderful when I see it."

He turned his head and pressed a kiss to her palm. "I wish I *had* been your first."

"Well, you were, in a way," she confessed, so completely under his spell, she could hold nothing back. "I never reached a climax until tonight, and I'm so glad that it happened with you. You've made me complete as a woman. Given me faith in myself. I'm grateful to you for so many things, not just what you've taught me about the wine industry, or for bringing me here, and taking the time to show me this beautiful city, but for what you've taught me about myself."

Still buried inside her, he turned on his side and cradled her next to his powerful body. "I am the grateful one, my lovely Arlene. I wish there was time for us to learn more about one another. If so, we might discover—"

"Hush." She covered his lips with her fingertips, knowing well that promises made in the warm aftermath of loving tended to fall apart in the colder light of day. "I wish it, too, but things are what they are. I don't want to look ahead to next week, or next month. I want to savor every second of the time we have *now*, so that, when it's over, I remember only how good it was between us."

"I will make it good for you," he declared huskily, sweeping his hand up her back. "I will make it perfect."

She drifted to sleep on that promise, lulled by the comforting warmth of his embrace and the soothing stroke of his big, strong hand. She didn't move again until early light pierced the room and she opened her eyes to find him spread-eagled on his half of the bed, leaving her lonely on hers.

Her mouth felt swollen, she ached in places not mentioned in polite society, and the musky scent of sex clung to her skin. Not that she minded; they were the prized mementos of an unforgettable night.

The morning after, though, could be a treacherous time, and her first instinct was to sneak away to her own bathroom and repair some of the damage before he awoke. But she couldn't resist taking a minute to commit to memory how he looked in sleep, with his lean jaw softened by the dark smudge of new beard growth, and his hair falling in undisciplined strands over his forehead.

Somewhere within the long, elegant lines, broad shoulders and deep chest of the mature man lurked the faint image of the boy he'd once been, before the years had sculpted him to hard masculine perfection. The thought brought a different ache, one that struck at her heart. If things had been different and she'd been the kind who'd measure up as his ideal wife, she might have had his child. A boy who looked like him, with the same black hair and thick eyelashes and olive skin.

Suddenly he opened his eyes and caught her staring. "*Ciao*, again," he said, bathing her in a sleepy smile. "Good morning, *cara mia*."

"Oh, my!" Blushing, she tried to turn away. "I didn't want you to see me looking like this."

"And how is that?"

She hunched her shoulders and tried to poke her mussed-up hair into some sort of order. A useless undertaking. It defied any attempt to lie flat and behave. "Morning-after messy," she muttered.

He slung an arm over her hips and nuzzled her spine, from her nape to the small of her back, then all the way up again. "On you, I like morning-after messy. I like it very much."

And I like you, she thought, her entire body vibrating in sensory delight. *Far more than is good for either of us.*

He nibbled her earlobe. "I have two pieces of very good news for you. First, I'm taking you out for breakfast. Second, we have an hour before we must leave." He pulled her around to face him and kissed her. Very, very thoroughly. "How do you suggest we pass the time?"

It was pretty clear what he had in mind. He was powerfully aroused. So big and hard, she couldn't take her eyes off him.

He cupped her breasts and wove delicious circles around her nipples with his thumbs. "It's quite all right to touch, *cara*," he murmured. "I don't bite."

She'd never been so bold with a man. Never had the opportunity, and wasn't sure exactly how to go about it. But he, sensing her hesitation, took her hand and closed it around him. "It's your fault I'm in this shape," he continued in that same mesmerizing tone. "It's only fair you do something about it, don't you think?"

Instinctively she clasped him tighter. He was

smooth as silk, the conformation of him so stunningly beautiful that she forgot to be bashful. To give back a little of the pleasure he so unstintingly brought to her was her only thought—if, indeed, her brain was able to formulate anything as structured as thought, when she was dissolving under his continued ministrations.

Spanning both her breasts with one hand and squeezing gently, he slid the other between her legs and found the liquid core of her. "Yes," he breathed, fixing her in a heavy-lidded gaze as she started to tremble. "Just so, my lovely. Show me how much you like the way we are together."

Oh, "like" didn't begin to cover it! With every word, every glance, every erotic suggestion and touch, he drew her more deeply under his spell. Left her so mindless with desire that she cared about nothing but that moment. The ramifications of investing so much of herself in this man, what it meant—a future too bleak to contemplate without him in it, the heartache of finding love at last, only to have it unrequited—those she pushed aside, to be dealt with another day. For now, all that mattered was living to the fullest every thrilling second of the present, and weaving it into a tapestry of memories so vivid, time could never fade them.

Morning-after love, she discovered, was different from that inspired by moonlight. It came cloaked in leisure, in the easy melding of two bodies already familiar with each other. The tension built slowly, sweetly, a dazzling raindrop of passion sliding smoothly to the edge of reason and clinging precariously until it could hold on no longer and shattered into a million rainbows.

Afterward, he carried her into his shower. They soaped each other, washing away the scent of love, then wrapped themselves in big bath sheets. She sat on the deck surrounding the bathtub and dried her hair, all the time watching in dreamy fascination as he shaved; admiring the easy play of muscles in his back and arms, his gleaming olive skin and dark hair. He stood with his long, strong legs splayed, his hips tilted forward a little as he concentrated on his task, completely at ease in her company.

Sliding once again into the addictive world of make-believe, she thought, This is what marriage to him would be like—the unselfconscious sharing of small intimacies and always, never far from the surface, the knowledge of deeper intimacies to come.

Pointless thinking, certainly, because the plain fact was, Arlene Russell and Domenico Silvaggio d'Avalos came from such vastly different worlds that they might as well live on separate planets. Take away the glamour of the moment, the simmering fire of sexual awareness between them, and they were left with no common meeting place; no happy medium that would allow them to honor their commitments and not sacrifice what they shared together.

He splashed water over his face and mopped it dry. "Time to get a move on, *cara*," he said, putting an end to her dismal conclusions. "Make sure you wear something comfortable. We have a distance to go before breakfast."

Carpe diem, Arlene, she told herself bracingly. Stop wishing for the moon. Just seize the day and relish every moment!

She thought he'd take her to a neighborhood bistro within walking distance of the hotel. In fact, he took her by hot air balloon to a château in the country. His driver dropped them off next to an open field just south of the city, and before she could catch her breath, let alone decide if she was ready for the experience, she found herself bundled into the big wicker basket, and they were lifting off the ground.

"Your first ride?" the pilot, Simon, inquired, laughing at her white knuckled grip on the waist-high rim of the basket as the ground crew released the last line, and he fired the burners into the dome of the nylon envelope to gain more altitude and catch the prevailing wind.

And possibly my last! she thought. How could such a fragile contraption be safe?

But her apprehension faded as they drifted serenely over the sun-dappled landscape. Because they traveled with the wind, she was comfortably warm. Domenico stood beside her, his arm at her waist, and that was all she needed to feel safe.

For an hour, they sailed over sleepy villages, quiet country roads and lazy winding rivers. The autumn foliage glowed bright yellow and burnt orange in the early morning sun. She saw a woman hanging laundry on a line, children on their way to school who stopped to wave, a fox running beside a hedge, rabbits scurrying to hide in a patch of bushes. When they passed over farmland, the pilot used a different technique, somehow reducing the noise made by the burners to avoid frightening the livestock grazing in the fields.

Finally they cleared a wooded area and there below lay the château, its stone facade perfectly reflected in the surface of the lake fronting it. Built along classical lines, with a steep mansard roof, tall chimneys and long, elegant windows, it stood at the end of a long avenue lined with ancient chestnut trees, amid acres of gently rolling land.

Deer leaped for the cover of the trees as the big red and blue striped balloon made a slow descent. "Hold on tight," Domenico warned, bracing her firmly at his side. "Even with a pilot as experienced as ours, landings can sometimes be a little rough."

Simon brought the craft down so skillfully and gradually, however, that the basket bumped gently over the grass until the ground crew with whom he'd been in radio contact was able to bring it to a final stop and hold it steady.

She climbed out and was surprised when one of the crew produced a hamper containing a bottle of champagne and crystal flutes. "It's customary to raise a toast at the end of a flight," Domenico explained, accepting two glasses and passing one to her.

But Arlene hardly needed champagne. She was content to drink in the perfection of the scene before her. Timeless and dignified, the château rose up against a sky tinted the pale, cool blue of approaching winter. The sun glinted on its many windows and cast sharply defined shadows over its lawns. A hush hung over the land, broken only by an occasional burst of birdsong.

Leaving her wine untouched, she wandered away from the men, lost in her own thoughts. The peaceful setting spoke to her in ways Toronto never had, and brought home to her in a flash of insight one of the reasons she'd been so quick to accept her inheritance. She'd lived in the city most of her life, but it had taken a great-uncle she'd never met to teach her she was a country woman at heart.

Domenico came up behind her and wound his arms around her waist. "So what do you think?" he asked, resting his chin on her hair.

"That it's the most beautiful place I've ever seen. It'll inspire me when I tackle restoring my house on the lake, though mine will never be as grand as this." She turned her head and pressed a kiss to his cheek. "Thank you for bringing me here, Domenico, and for all the other wonderful memories you've given me."

Whatever he'd been about to reply, he suddenly changed his mind, and tucking her hand in the crook of his elbow, said instead, "Let's go inside. You must be starving and I know I am."

They walked along a gravel path that wound around to the château's main entrance where a butler of sorts waited to greet them. Tall, slender and silver-haired, he was as elegant as the house itself.

He ushered them inside to a graciously appointed room overlooking the lake. Rich cream silk draperies hung at the windows, the floors gleamed with a patina resulting from centuries of polishing, and the antique furniture might have come from a museum. But more than all that, it was the single table for two, set next to the fire roaring in the huge stone fireplace, which put paid to Arlene's perception that Domenico had brought her to some exclusive hotel catering to the very wealthy.

"What is this place?" she whispered, the minute the butler left them alone.

"A country house," he said.

"Whose?"

"Mine."

Her jaw dropped.

He laughed. "Why the surprise, *cara*?"

"Well, for a start, you live in Sardinia."

"Most of the time, yes. But when I want solitude, I sometimes come here."

"So who looks after the place the rest of the time?"

"Emile, whom you just met, and his wife, Christianne. Also their three sons. They oversee the estate for me, with hired help from the village when it's needed."

"I thought you were devoted to your family."

"I am. But as I already told you, we don't live in each other's back pockets. I have my retreats, and they have theirs."

Retreats, she wondered. *As in more than one?*

"Now you look shocked, *cara*. Does that mean you don't approve?"

Still trying to come to grips with what she'd learned, she said, "It's not a question of approving, so much as being taken aback. I know people who have a place in the country, but that usually means a cabin or a cottage, not something a French king might once have lived in."

"I believe the original château did once belong to royalty," he said offhandedly, as if owning a chunk of history was no more important than buying a new pair of shoes, "but what you see now was built in the mid-nineteenth century."

"How did you come by it?"

"I heard that it was on the market." He shrugged. "It took my fancy, so I bought it."

At that point, the butler, wheeling in their meal on an elaborate serving wagon, put an end to the conversation. When it resumed, over a delectable clafoutis made with tiny black cherries, they talked about other things, specifically what she should expect the next day, when the convention began.

"It will be tiring, and very intense. Unfortunately I can't be with you all the time because of meetings I scheduled several weeks ago, but I'll introduce you to people I know, and we'll meet for meals."

"Don't worry about me," she told him. "I'll be fine on my own and certainly don't expect you to hold my hand all the time."

"Not even if I want to?" he said, dazzling her with his smile.

Please don't be so charming! she wanted to tell

him. *Don't make me fall in love with you any more than I already have.*

When they'd finished eating, he showed her other parts of the house: the ballroom with its glittering crystal chandeliers, the spacious, elegant reception rooms; the upstairs suites with their claw-foot bathtubs, four-poster beds and carved armoires; the dining hall with its mirrored walls and long, polished table.

Finally after a visit to the kitchen to thank Emile and Christianne for their hospitality, they took a walk outside, and Arlene could see how it would take three grown men to oversee the grounds and keep them looking so pristine. Nothing marred the surface of the ornamental pond. The cobbled courtyard was swept free of leaves, the rose garden neatly pruned ready for winter.

But it was at their last stop in the greenhouse—the *orangerie*, Domenico called it—that she realized there was a dimension to him that had nothing to do with wealth. A man worked at one end, painstakingly washing the leaves of a lemon tree with a small paintbrush. At their approach, he turned, and she saw at once that he had Down syndrome.

Recognizing Domenico, he broke into a beaming smile and burst into speech, the words falling over themselves in his delight. Although her French was passably good, she couldn't understand everything he said, but Domenico had no trouble at all. After introducing him as Emile and Christianne's eldest son, Jean, he focused all his attention on what the man was so eager to tell him. Arlene didn't have to understand the words being exchanged to realize that Domenico ranked only slightly lower than God in Jean's estimation, and that keeping the greenhouse in perfect order for his idol was his passion in life.

They spent perhaps half an hour with him, during which time he showed Arlene his prized citrus trees and presented her with a sweet-scented lemon blossom. Although Domenico accompanied them, he left it up to her to make what she could of the conversation. Only when Emile came to announce that their driver was waiting did he step in and, counteracting Jean's disappointment that their visit had been so short, brought it to a close with enviable diplomacy.

"Thank you for being so patient with Jean," he said, taking her hand as the chauffeur drove the car down the long avenue of chestnut trees and took the road back to the city.

She looked at the fragile lemon blossom resting in her lap. "How could I not be, Domenico? He is a sweet and gentle soul."

"Not everyone sees him or his brother that way."

"His brother has Down syndrome, too?"

"Yes. Emile and Christianne desperately wanted children, but couldn't have their own, so they decided to adopt. When they learned how difficult it was for older children, especially those with a handicap, to find placement with parents who would love them despite their difficulties, they decided it was God's will that they give their love to such a child. Jean was seven when they brought him home. Two years later, they adopted Léon."

"And the youngest?"

Domenico smiled. "God changed His mind. Christianne fell pregnant when Léon was five, and gave birth to a healthy baby boy. Hilaire will turn forty in December."

"How did they all end up here, or were they already in residence when you bought the place?"

"No. I heard of them through an associate. There'd been several very unpleasant incidents in their village, which is some distance from here. The details aren't important. It's enough to say the entire family's lives were made miserable because Jean and Léon were different.

"They needed a fresh start, some place where they wouldn't be at the mercy of ignorant louts. I happened to have such a place, and I needed staff to run it."

"That's a beautiful story," she said, her voice

cracking with emotion. "And you're a remarkable man."

"There's nothing remarkable about lending a hand when it's needed. What's money for, after all, if it can't be put to good use?"

"Not every man with money has your moral integrity, Domenico."

"Then I'd say he's bankrupt where it matters the most. The wealthy don't own exclusive rights to decency and kindness."

She shouldn't be surprised by his revelations, she thought. He'd done nothing but surprise her, from the moment they'd met.

They reached Paris just after two and spent a couple of hours in the Louvre museum, then toured the picturesque old streets of Montmartre before heading back to the Ritz around six o'clock.

After such a long, wonderful day, they decided against going out for dinner that night. Instead Domenico had a meal brought up to the suite. "Nothing too special, so don't feel you have to dress up," he told her, when she went to change her clothes. "In fact, be comfortable and wear your bathrobe."

"I will, if you will," she said mischievously.

He laughed. "I thought you'd never ask!"

To her, "nothing special" meant a hamburger or

pizza. She should have known better than to expect he'd think along such mundane lines. When she returned to the salon after her bath, she found a linen-draped table, with flowers, lighted candles and the hotel's signature sterling and china. On a cloth covered serving table were chafing dishes hidden under silver domes, and wine chilling in a silver ice bucket.

They dined on creamy wild mushroom soup, pheasant with poached pears, and strawberries dipped in chocolate. In Arlene's opinion, the only thing more delicious was Domenico in a bathrobe, with his hair still wet from the shower and his jaw freshly shaved.

"Has it been a good day?" he asked her, after the remains of the meal had been taken away and she sat curled up next to him on the sofa.

"Oh, very! But it's made me realize that although you know a great deal about me, I still know next to nothing about you."

"Not much mystery there, Arlene," he said. "I was born in the house where you had dinner with my family, got into all the trouble boys usually manage to get into, eventually grew up, went to the U.S. to study, earned a master's degree in viticulture and enology at California State University, then came home again and took over the family business because my father developed a heart condition that forced him into early retirement. That about covers it."

"I don't think so," she said, cataloging not just the events of that day, but all the others that made up the time she'd spent with him. "You're a lot more complex than you make yourself out to be. You just don't want to talk about it."

"Well, why would I, when I could be making love to you?" he whispered against her ear.

And just like that, she forgot everything but the sublime pleasure he so easily aroused in her. She didn't need to know anything else.

Or so she believed, at the time.

CHAPTER EIGHT

AT FIRST, it all went well enough. She woke up early on the Friday, eager to begin the day, eager to make him proud. She didn't dwell on the fact that, on Sunday, she'd be saying goodbye to him, because perhaps it wouldn't come to that. Perhaps what they shared was too glorious to be snuffed out, and instead of coming to an end, they'd find they were just beginning.

She dressed carefully, teaming one of her silk blouses in a subtle black and white pinstripe with the cranberry-red suit. She pinned up her hair in a neat coil, inserted her pearl stud earrings and stepped into her new black leather pumps with the smart two-inch heels.

The chauffeur stood waiting, with the engine purring and car door already held open, when she and Domenico came out of the hotel. Seated next to her in the back seat, he looked at once supremely relaxed and ultra-professional in a dark gray suit, white shirt and burgundy tie, with only the soft gleam of his gold cuff links and watch to soften their severity. A leather attaché case rested on the seat beside him.

She sat with her knees pressed together nervously and her handbag and a new notebook clutched to her breast. Now that the moment was almost upon her, she wasn't quite as sure of herself.

The mob scene when they arrived at the convention hall did nothing to boost her morale. Although Domenico had told her English would be the common language for all organized events, the babble of foreign tongues assaulting her was enough to send her running for the hills. She didn't belong in such a well-heeled, cosmopolitan gathering; couldn't even identify half the languages being spoken. Not that it mattered. She didn't know enough about viticulture to hold a conversation with anyone, anyway.

Domenico, of course, suffered no such qualms. Grasping her elbow, he steered her confidently through the crowd, which parted for him as if he were Moses commanding the Red Sea.

"Wait here," he ordered, depositing her next to a table overflowing with brochures. "I'll be right back." And promptly disappeared.

In fact, he was gone nearly fifteen minutes, during which time she pretended an interest in the first pamphlet she could lay hands on—which, she gathered from the address on the back, was written in Hungarian but might as well have been Swahili for all the good it did her.

"Sorry," he muttered, when he finally returned. "The trouble with events like this is that you can't avoid running into people you know."

She could. His was the only familiar face among hundreds.

"Here's your registration package," he went on, handing her an embossed binder beside which her spiral notebook looked pitifully inadequate. Program, pens, felt markers, paper, ministapler, calculator—the binder had it all. "Over breakfast, I'll mark the sessions you'll find most useful. You'll see there's a floor plan showing where each takes place. After we've eaten, we'll attend the keynote address together, then you'll be on your own until lunch. We'll meet back here at noon, but in case you're detained or can't find me, here's my cell phone number." He handed her a business card. "Tuck it some place handy."

And with that, they were off, caught up in the tide of humanity flowing toward the room where a buffet of brioches, croissants, coffee and juice waited. He had warned her it would be hectic. In fact, it was bedlam.

Somehow, though, she survived the morning,

managing not only to acquire much useful information, but also finding herself swept up in an enthusiasm generated by the conventioneers themselves. To hear them talk, the wine industry was the most thrilling and satisfying occupation in the world, and by lunchtime, she believed them.

When the sessions ended, she found Domenico already waiting for her at their appointed meeting place. Unfortunately he wasn't alone. The woman with him didn't quite hang around his neck like a second tie, but she made it very clear she'd like to.

"You survived," he said, his face lighting up in a smile when he saw Arlene. "How was it?"

"Incredible. I'm really fired up."

"That's what I want to hear." He took her arm and gave it a discreetly intimate squeeze as he introduced her to his companion. "Arlene, this is Ortensia Costanza, one of my neighbors in Sardinia. She and her family own a winery on the west coast of the island."

"A neighbor, *and* a friend," the woman corrected, her eyes skating over Arlene's cranberry suit as if she recognized it as one she herself had turned in to the consignment boutique in Alghero. Which was impossible, of course. She was at least four inches shorter than Arlene, with breasts twice the size. "A very *dear* friend, in fact. Shall we go into lunch, Domenico? Raffaello is saving us a table."

"By all means."

Deftly, he maneuvered Arlene into the huge dining room, and with a brief word of introduction to the other seven already seated, took his place next to her. The flamboyant Ortensia noticed, and was not pleased. Taking the only remaining vacant chair, she said, "I don't recall seeing you here before, *signorina*."

"No. I'm new to the business."

"Indeed." She allowed herself a small, malicious smile. "And Domenico's taken you under his wing, has he?"

"Yes."

"And exactly what is your area of interest?"

The same as yours, she felt like replying. *The difference is, I'm the one he's making love to every night.* "I don't have one," she said. "I'm quite literally starting from scratch."

Her admission sparked a flurry of interest among the others at the table, but conversation became more general as the meal progressed.

"You're on this afternoon, Domenico?" one woman inquired, and when he nodded, smiled at Arlene and said kindly, "You mustn't miss that, my dear. Domenico alone is worth the price of admission to this event. You'll learn more in two hours with him than a whole day with anyone else."

"Don't listen to Madeline," Domenico said,

with a laugh. "I pay her to say things like that. You'll do better to stick to the original plan."

"Certainly," the bosomy Ortensia chipped in. "The more basic, the better for someone like you. Domenico's presentation will be far too advanced."

Quite possibly so, but Arlene had no intention of missing it. Scanning her program, she made a note of when and where he'd take the podium.

The rest of the afternoon passed quickly and by the time she took her place in the room where he was to speak, she'd accumulated enough information on the pitfalls and rewards of getting a vineyard up and running that she could almost write a book for beginners.

The room was packed to capacity and she, seated well to the rear, felt comfortably inconspicuous. Domenico didn't notice her when he arrived, but she was instantly aware of him. The very second he strode through the door, a buzz of anticipation rippled over the audience. In a hall full of self-assured, successful entrepreneurs, more than half of them probably millionaires several times over, he stood just a little bit taller. Impossible to overlook, impossible to forget.

Ortensia Costanza had been right on one count, though. Most of his dissertation was far above Arlene's head, but she didn't care. It was enough to watch him, to listen to the rich cadence of his voice. To dream about the night ahead, when there'd be only the two of them, and everything he said, everything he did, would resonate within her.

But first, she discovered, there was the evening to get through.

"We're invited to a private dinner party," he told her, loosening his tie and stretching out his long legs in the back of the car, during the ride back to the Ritz. "I know you're exhausted, *cara*, and if you'd rather I go alone—"

"No," she said quickly. "I want to be with you."

He put his arm around her shoulders and pulled her close. "And I, with you—and no one else. But there are obligations in these affairs that can't go ignored."

"I understand, Domenico, really."

"It's not yet six o'clock, and we don't have to leave the suite until eight. You'll have time to unwind and take a nap."

Not likely, she thought. She wasn't about to waste precious time napping. She could catch up on her sleep all next week, if necessary. For now, a hot bath would be enough to revive her.

But her feet were killing her, and once back in her room and she'd shucked off her shoes and stripped naked, she changed her mind. The bed looked awfully inviting, and lying down for half an hour didn't seem like such a bad idea, after all.

Snug though she felt beneath the comforter, she hardly expected to sleep, not with her mind in overdrive after the stimulation of the day. But she must have dropped off because the next thing she knew, Domenico was murmuring soft and low in her ear, "Wake up, my lovely."

Her room was dim, lit only by the lamplight spilling through the open door from the salon. "It's time to get ready?" she mumbled, her voice rusty with sleep.

His hand lay cool against the swell of her breast, but his mouth on hers was hot and demanding. "I didn't say that," he breathed, and slid into her, a lovely, slow, sensuous invasion that ran through her blood like warm honey.

There was nothing quite like love as an aperitif, to neutralize the unpleasant effect of finding Ortensia Costanza was among the guests at the private supper club where the dinner was held. Arriving on Domenico's arm, Arlene positively floated on a cloud of euphoria. Her black velvet dinner dress was exactly right for the occasion, a statement in sophistication that required no adornment beyond Gail's crystal earrings.

Naturally enough, much of the conversation revolved around business. Markets came under scrutiny; international wine awards were discussed, future trends predicted. But they were, for the most part, a cultured, mannerly group of people, and didn't forget the newcomer in their midst.

Encouraged by their interest, she told them how she'd come by her vineyard. Apart from Ortensia, who affected utter boredom with the subject, they peppered her with questions and advice.

"You've done well by your distant relative," one man, a fiftyish American, observed as the party was breaking up. "That area of British Columbia is garnering huge respect worldwide for the quality of grape it's producing. We in the Napa Valley will have to look to our laurels."

His wife nodded agreement. "Jimmy's right. Everyone who's anyone in this business is buzzing about your neck of the woods. You're a lucky woman."

"Lucky and charming," her husband said. "It's been an honor to meet you, Arlene. Where did you find this young woman, Domenico?"

"I didn't. She found me," he said, bathing her in a smile that made her toes curl inside their borrowed silver evening pumps.

Ortensia, who'd remained silent until that point, suddenly spoke up, her voice as sour as her expression. "You always did have a talent being in exactly the right place at exactly the right time when some poor soul needs you, Domenico."

At that, a brief uncomfortable silence filled the room, before he replied. "And you, my dear Ortensia," he said, his tone of steely disfavor erasing any scrap of affection from the endearment, "never have learned when to keep your unasked-for opinions to yourself."

Then dismissing her, he turned to their hosts with an apologetic smile and a murmured word of thanks for the evening. Taking their cue from him, the others dispelled the lingering tension in a spate of goodbyes, and made their way to the fleet of cars waiting to take them back to their various hotels.

"That was unpleasant, and I apologize," Domenico said, tucking Arlene's cape around her shoulders against the brisk October night as they walked the few yards to where his driver was parked. "Ortensia is a spoiled, self-indulgent woman who is used to being the center of attention. I'm afraid she didn't take kindly to your upstaging her, but please don't take it personally. She'd have been just as disagreeable had it been any other woman."

He was wrong, Arlene thought. Ortensia was more than spoiled, she was eaten alive with jealousy because she wanted Domenico for herself. And that, in Arlene's opinion, made her attack very personal indeed.

* * *

The clock showed it was after three in the morning. Worn out from the hectic day and long evening, Arlene lay fast asleep in his bed, but Domenico paced the salon floor, wide-awake and irritable. Most of the people who'd attended the dinner party were good friends he saw only once a year, and always before, he'd looked forward to a long, stimulating visit with them. Tonight had been different. He'd chafed at its leisurely progress, his thoughts obsessed with the fact that he was running out of time with Arlene and could ill afford to waste four precious hours.

He'd thought he had all the answers where she was concerned, that when their time together came to an end, he could walk away from her and not look back. She was an innocent who'd been thrown by an unknown relative into an unknown situation, and by sheer luck she'd ended up on his doorstep, seeking his help. That didn't make her his responsibility, he told himself for what seemed like the hundredth time. He'd given her the benefit of his advice and experience. The rest was up to her. She'd either make a go of her vineyard, or she wouldn't.

Or was *he* the innocent, to have believed he could play with fire and not get burned? He'd had no thought of a permanent involvement with her when first they met. Had been certain the attraction between them was a passing thing: Pleasurable, of course, just like others before her, but never meant to last.

He'd felt secure in knowing he was expert at ending such affairs gracefully. There'd be no emotional meltdowns when it came time to say goodbye. They'd go their separate ways with good memories and no hard feelings, no lingering regret, no deep abiding sense of loss.

So when had it all begun to change? The first time he kissed her? When he'd almost seduced her in the front seat of his car? When he'd stopped having sex with her, and instead started making love to her? Had it begun the day they met and a worm of jealousy had poisoned him because he thought she'd come to Sardinia with another man? Or had it taken Ortensia Costanza to make him realize that, as far as Arlene was concerned, he was in so far over his head, he hadn't a hope of extricating himself?

He didn't have the answer. The only thing he knew for sure was that he wasn't immune, after all, to the weaknesses he'd witnessed in his friends. The confused mass of emotion she aroused in him left him as susceptible as the next man, and no more able to separate his life into neat compartments, than he could command the sun not to rise every morning.

She preyed on his mind, night and day. He was

worried about her, afraid for her. She faced at least four years of backbreaking labor before she could expect to see a return on her vineyard. With her limited knowledge, and probably limited resources, too, the pitfalls of the undertaking were huge and could ruin her both financially and mentally.

From his perspective, she'd been rejected enough by her monster of a mother, and he was filled with a fierce, burning desire to make sure that no one ever hurt her again. He wanted to protect her. Be part of her life, a strong shoulder for her to lean on when she needed it. And in his book, all that added up to only one thing: he'd fallen in love with her. Except "added up" didn't quite fit because, contrary to what he'd always believed, it wasn't a mathematical equation arrived at by logic and conclusion. It was irrational, impractical and bloody inconvenient!

Dio, where was his legendary cool detachment when he needed it most?

"Domenico?" Her voice, soft with sleep, whispered to him across the room, and spinning on his heel, he found her standing in the bedroom doorway. "What's wrong?"

"Nothing. I'm having trouble sleeping, that's all."

She'd put on the shirt he'd worn to dinner. It swamped her slender frame. The sleeves hung inches below her hands, the tail almost to her knees. Her skin was rosy, her hair a silken sun-streaked tangle, and she looked adorable.

"Go back to bed, Arlene," he said brusquely. He had things to work out in his head, and that wouldn't happen with her making further inroads on his emotions.

"Not without you," she said, coming to him and resting her hands between the lapels of his bathrobe, quite literally putting her finger on the heart of the matter. "I miss you."

"Arlene…please!" In an agony of indecision, of a need that floored him, he grasped her wrists and pushed her away. "Just go!"

She shook her head. "Not until you tell me what's really bothering you."

"Ortensia," he said, latching on to the first thought that sprang to mind. "I'm furious with her. She was an embarrassment tonight—a disgrace to Sardinia with her churlish behavior toward you. There's no telling what next might have come out of her mouth, if the party hadn't ended when it did."

It wasn't a complete lie. He'd wanted to throttle the woman for making Arlene the target of her frustrated resentment. He knew she'd set her sights on him, and he'd tried to let her know as diplomatically as possible that she was never going to succeed. His mistake! He should have spoken bluntly, a long time ago. Perhaps then, tonight's unfortunate scene could have been avoided.

"I don't care about Ortensia," Arlene said softly, untying the belt at his waist and pressing a damp kiss to his chest. "I care about you. Come back to bed, Domenico, and let me show you how much."

She mesmerized him with her artless seduction. Against his better judgment, he let her lead him back to the bedroom. She stripped off his bathrobe and as he stood there, naked and painfully aroused, she sank to her knees and took him in her mouth.

He almost came. So nearly lost control that he yanked her to her feet with an abrupt curse.

"Oh!" she breathed, collapsing against him on a forlorn sigh. "I want to please you, but I've never done that before, and—"

If she had, he'd have killed the man! "Stop it!" he said harshly. "For the love of God, Arlene, stop apologizing for not being perfect!"

And driven beyond reason by the desire running rampant through him, he ripped his shirt off her body, pushed her down on the bed and drove into her. Furiously. Once, twice, three times. The fourth time, she peaked, gloving him so tightly and sweetly that he could hold back no longer. Without thought of contraception or the possible consequences of such an oversight, he gave in to the forces tearing him apart, and spilled free inside her in a powerful rush.

He was lost, and he knew it.

They didn't make it to the Saturday program. Wrapped in each other's arms, they slept late, stirring only when the sun was high. They ordered breakfast in bed, vowing to catch the afternoon sessions, but raspberry-stuffed crepes and mimosas weren't enough to satisfy their appetite, and somehow the morning wasted away in slow explorations more delicious than anything the hotel chef could hope to produce. Still insatiable for each other, they made love again in the deep marble bathtub, their bodies slick and eager, awash in sensation and soap.

Eventually they dressed and made it out to the street for a final tour of Paris. There'd be no time tomorrow; she was meeting Gail early in the morning for their eleven-thirty flight to Toronto. Domenico took her to the top of the Eiffel Tower, and showed her the elegant shops favored by the glitterati along the Rue du Fauborg Saint-Honoré and Avenue Montaigne. Over her objections, he bought her a cashmere shawl and bottle of perfume at Hermès.

Then, as the shadows lengthened, they climbed the hill to Sacré Coeur, and sat on the cathedral steps, eating ham sandwiches he'd picked up at one of the many cafés in the area. The air was brisk, with a hint of frost, but she didn't need her cape, tailored wool slacks and suede boots to be comfortable. Domenico's smile, his touch, his voice warmed her from the inside out.

Strolling back through the Latin Quarter, they browsed the many artworks displayed in the streets of Montmartre. When she stopped to admire an oil painting, a tiny unframed canvas no more than six inches square, showing the city at sunset, again nothing would do but that Domenico negotiate a price with the artist. A short while later, he spotted a handsomely bound book on the history of Paris, filled with photographs of the places they'd visited together, and presented her with that, too.

"You've already done so much for me," she protested. "Please don't feel you have to buy me gifts, as well."

But, "No one should leave Paris without at least a couple of souvenirs," he said.

Because he was to receive an award, they had to attend that night's banquet, to be held at the Hotel George V, and in a way, she was glad they wouldn't be alone. It would be too easy for misery to creep in and spoil their last night together. Better to be among a crowd; to dance with him and weave a few more golden strands into the magic they'd spun together.

She was glad she'd succumbed to the temptation of the beaded celadon evening gown, even if she never had occasion to wear it again. It was worth every euro she'd spent on it, just to see Domenico's face when she joined him in the salon, and hear him exclaim softly, "You are beautiful!"

"And so are you," she said, reaching up to smooth the lapel of his black dinner jacket. "I'm the luckiest woman in the world to be spending this night with you."

For a few hours, she continued to bask in his attention. He was the perfect escort, the sexiest, most handsome man in the world, and he was all hers—until she happened to go to the ladies' room and disturb a conversation taking place among half a dozen women from last night's dinner party, among them Ortensia Costanza.

"…broke and besotted," she heard Ortensia sneer.

"She's ripe for the plucking, certainly," someone else agreed.

Then six pairs of eyes turned startled gazes Arlene's way as the door swung closed behind her. "Am I interrupting?" she asked hesitantly. A foolish question, since she obviously was. But five of them fell over themselves to deny it as they pretended to fix their already immaculate hairdos and touch up their already perfect lipstick.

"No, no, of course not! We were just talking about…"

"The grape harvest this year."

But they weren't. *She's* ripe for the picking is what Arlene had heard, and given their agitation at discovering her suddenly in their midst, who else could they have been referring to but her? Except what did she have that anyone would want?

"Really," she said steadily.

"Yes! But it's so nice to see you again, Arlene."

"Indeed yes. What a lovely gown!"

"Oh, absolutely! The color was created with you in mind."

"How are you enjoying the evening?" the oldest of the six, inquired, concern evident in her kind brown eyes. "Domenico's taking good care of you, is he?"

Arlene smiled. "He's being quite wonderful."

Ortensia stepped forward, five inches taller tonight in her spike-heeled shoes. Diamonds the size of sugar cubes dangled from her ears. Another even larger gem graced her right forefinger. Her well-endowed bosom swelled provocatively above the top of her strapless red satin gown. "And you don't have a clue why, do you, you poor little *micina*?"

"Ortensia, please!" one of the women begged.

She dismissed the warning with a toss of her head. "She deserves to know."

Do not dignify that remark by asking her to explain it, Arlene ordered herself, and promptly said, "Exactly what do you mean, Ortensia? Are you suggesting he's merely pretending to enjoy my company?"

"Oh, he enjoys it," she replied. "He enjoys it very much—for a couple of reasons. First, it makes him feel good to know he's saved another lost soul."

"Be quiet this instant, Ortensia!" the brown-eyed woman interrupted sharply. "You've gone far enough, and I refuse to stand by and watch you destroy another hapless woman whose only sin is that she's come between you and the man you've been trying to snare for more years than I care to count."

"Then feel free to leave, but I intend to set this poor creature straight. You," she continued, turning her inimical gaze on Arlene again, "assume he's showering you with attention because he finds you fascinating and irresistible. But the truth is, you don't really exist for him, not as a *person* or a *woman.*"

"I haven't a clue what you're talking about," Arlene said flatly, even as the prickle of apprehension crawling over her skin told her she'd be better off not knowing.

A sigh gusted past Ortensia's pouty lips. "*Dio*, are you blind? Do you not see you're simply another stray he's taken on, just like those flea-bitten children from the slums of Paris that he lets run wild at his château every summer, and the orphans he sponsors in Bolivia, and Africa, and Romania?"

"I don't believe you," Arlene said numbly.

Ortensia snorted and threw out her hands to her frozen audience. "Explain it to her! Tell her she's not the first, and she won't be the last! That he's known as Signor Humanitarian in some circles because he's forever showering the rejects of this world with his largesse, no matter where he happens to find them."

Mutely Arlene turned to them, and saw how they couldn't meet her gaze.

"It's true, he does involve himself in many... worthy charities," one of them finally admitted. "He likes to help where he can, but, Arlene, that's not to say you're just another project to him. It's obvious to all of us that his interest in you is much more personal."

"*Dio*, you think? Is it possible I've misread the signs?" Ortensia clapped a hand to her bosom with dramatic flair and swung her gaze to Arlene again. "Am I indeed mistaken, *cara?* Could it be that the untouchable Domenico Silvaggio d'Avalos has abandoned his usual routine of merely opening his wallet, and has finally unlocked his heart, as well?"

Not about to let the woman know how rattled she was, Arlene traded stares with her. "I don't pretend to be his spokesperson. Why don't you ask him yourself, since you're so interested?"

Ortensia's eyes flashed with triumph. "I don't need to, Arlene!" she sneered. "I know a lame duck when I see one, almost as well as I know Domenico. He's the first to ride to the rescue in a crisis, and if it happens to involve a woman still young enough to have all her own teeth, well, so much the better. He is, after all, a red-blooded Sardinian of the first order. The only difference between you and dozens before you is that he's looking to be rewarded with more than just a roll in the hay."

"He's after my vast fortune, you mean? My goodness, he's in for a big disappointment!"

She spoke lightly, desperate to hide her growing dismay, but Ortensia wasn't deceived. *"Idiota!"* she spat with transparent contempt. "Your wealth is nothing more than pocket change to him. It's your land that he covets. Seducing you just happened to be the easiest way to get it, and if you haven't yet figured that out, you're not just naive, you're downright feeble-minded."

"All right, that's enough!" Snapping closed her evening bag, the brown-eyed woman manacled Ortensia by the wrist and frog-marched her to the door. "This ends now."

The four left behind looked at Arlene from shifty, sympathetic eyes. "Pay no attention," one finally muttered, edging toward the door. "Ortensia is a loose cannon at the best of times."

Perhaps so, but she'd scored a direct hit—and Arlene had only herself to blame. She was the one who'd confided everything about herself to Domenico, right down to the last details of her inheritance.

...broke and besotted!

She's ripe for the plucking....

At least she hadn't told him she loved him. And she never would.

Infuriated as much by her own foolishness as Ortensia's spitefully accurate portrayal, Arlene rallied her shredded pride. "No apologies, please, and no explanations. I'm well aware what kind of woman Ortensia is."

After all, hadn't Domenico pretty much spelled it out, just last night? *There's no telling what next might come out of her mouth....*

Well, how about the truth, Domenico? she thought bitterly.

CHAPTER NINE

PREPARED to do whatever it took to get through the remainder of that endless, agonizing evening, Arlene pinned a brilliant smile on her face, returned to the table where he sat waiting for her, and acted out the charade of a woman having the time of her life.

She'd rubbed shoulders with millionaires before, even if it had been only in her capacity as legal secretary to the law firm's senior partner, but she was smart, she was observant and she knew how they behaved. Consequently she acted witty and charming, looked suitably interested in whatever conversation happened to be taking place, laughed in all the right places and generally shimmered just like her dress. Domenico's last memory of her would not be the pathetic nobody he'd temporarily elevated to his rarified level, but a woman well able to hold her own, regardless of the society in which she found herself.

Still, she paid a terrible price. Every smile,

every bright, amusing remark found its origin in the bitter taste of disillusionment.

There's nothing remarkable about lending a hand when it's needed, he'd said, not two days earlier. *What's money for, after all, if it can't be put to good use? A man's material wealth doesn't preclude his right to decency and compassion.*

Although he hadn't exactly lied to her, he'd deceived her anyway by not spelling out all that he'd meant by that, but what hurt the most was knowing that she was the architect of her own misery. She should have said "no" to him a long time ago. Instead she'd ignored the signs posted along the way and walked blindly into a fool's paradise.

She'd climbed into his bed, even though he'd never said a word to make her believe he was interested in anything more than a temporary distraction; a fling spiced with unforgettable sex. After all, he was, as Ortensia had pointed out with succinct venom, a normal, red-blooded man. He was kind, and he was generous—in Arlene's case, donating his body as well as his considerable expertise in other areas. And he'd asked nothing in return, most especially not that she fall in love with him. She'd done that all by herself.

But he would never know she was broken inside. If she couldn't have his love, she wasn't about to settle for his pity.

By the time the evening dragged to a close, her face ached from its perpetual smile. All she wanted was for the pain to end; to leave Paris behind and to forget there'd ever been a tall, dark Sardinian who'd broken her heart. But first, there was the night to get through, and Domenico made it very plain that, for him, it was far from over.

"You were magnificent tonight, *cara*," he murmured, sweeping her cape from her shoulders the very second they set foot in the suite, and sewing a seam of tiny, exquisite kisses along the curve of her shoulder. "I could barely contain my impatience to be alone with you."

"Nor I with you," she said, injecting just the right degree of regret into the words, "but I'm so worn out that all I really want is to sleep."

"And you shall," he said, gliding the zipper of her dress smoothly down her spine. "In my arms, where you belong."

"Domenico...!" she objected on a sigh, but her protestations were drowned out by the whisper of fabric sliding away from her body until only his hands lay next to her skin.

The beguiling mists of passion closed around her, robbing her of the will to resist. She lifted her face for his kiss. Let her arms steal around his neck.

"Still too tired?" he murmured, and when she shook her head, unable to deny him, he carried her to his bed and stripped off his own clothes. Aligning his body with hers, he buried himself inside her. And with each deep, slow thrust, he stole a little more of her soul.

She tried to remain detached; to protect her grieving heart by being an observer, not a participant. But he knew her weaknesses and exploited them without mercy. Just when she thought she would scream for the exquisite agony he inflicted, he made a sound in his throat, low and guttural, and in a lightning move, rolled onto his back and positioned her so that she sat astride him.

Cupping her bottom, he pinned her against him in an attempt to halt the tide threatening to sweep them both past the point of no return. "Be still, my love, and make this moment last," he begged, sweat beading his brow.

She wished it could be so, but she'd been taken prisoner by a demon within herself; become the victim of a need so unappeasable, it would settle for nothing but immediate and total surrender. Fight it as she might, the tension coiled tighter within her, became unbearable, until she shattered into a thousand glittering prisms. Into stardust. Into ecstasy.

He tensed beneath her. Muttered her name once, drawing it out like a plea. Her vision filmed with tears, she looked down at him and thought she had never seen such tortured beauty in a man.

She wished she dared say the unthinkable; wished she could tell him she loved him. But they weren't words he wanted to hear. All she could give him was release from his self-imposed prison. Which she did, leaning back and tilting her hips in a tiny, imperative thrust that sent him soaring into oblivion.

"Look what you do to me," he ground out on a labored breath, when at last he could compose himself. "You destroy me and make me come when I would hold back forever if I could, buried to the hilt in your sleek and willing flesh."

"Forever" wasn't part of the plan, though, and soon enough darkness gave way to the gray of a new dawn. Arlene had slept not a wink. Had used the passing hours to plan her farewell. There would be no tears, no clinging, no lamenting. Whatever the cost, she would hold herself together long enough to make a dignified exit.

Easing herself carefully from his bed, she stole to her own room, stopping in the salon just long enough to scoop up her evening gown and other items from last night. Stuffing them into her suitcase, she took the clothes she'd wear for traveling, and locked herself in her bathroom. Within the hour, she was bathed, dressed and looking amazingly self-possessed, considering she was falling apart inside.

He was already up and waiting for her when she left her bedroom for the last time. Freshly shaved, and with his dark hair brushed severely in place, he looked solemn as an undertaker in black trousers and black turtleneck sweater. "We have time for breakfast before we leave for the airport," he said.

But she'd anticipated this might be what he had in mind, and had her answer ready. "No need for you to do that," she said cheerfully, even as her heart began to splinter. "For a start, I arranged to meet Gail for breakfast."

"In that case, I'll call for my car and the three of us—"

"No, Domenico," she cut in, hanging on to her resolve with the desperation of a drowning woman. "No car, and no breakfast for three. I'm not big on lengthy farewells, so let's make it short, sweet and final, right here and right now."

"But, *cara*, what's the rush? I hoped we'd have time to talk about—"

"We've said everything there is to say. All that's left is for me to tell you again how deeply I appreciate all you've done for me."

Sounding baffled, hurt even, he said, "At least let me walk you down to the lobby."

And prolong the agony? "No."

He caught her hand. Inched her closer. "You really mean this to be goodbye?"

"Yes."

He framed her face between his hands. His breath winnowed over her hair. His beautiful blue eyes bored into hers. "It doesn't have to be."

"Yes, Domenico, it does," she said, because being near him, having him touch her, just intensified the agony. "We crossed paths for a little while, and although it was wonderful while it lasted, it was…"

She floundered, at a loss. To denigrate what they'd shared was more than she could bring herself to do. It had been too glorious. It had touched her too deeply.

"What was it, Arlene?" he inquired, the edge of steel in his voice echoed in the sudden winter chill of his eyes.

"Just a…an autumn fling." She shrugged. "It's over now. You have your life and I have mine, and we both know they're worlds apart, so let's not pretend otherwise."

He fixed her in a long, inscrutable gaze. "You're right," he finally said. "Long distance relationships have never appealed to me. Better to make a clean break now. Neither of us would be happy with an occasional weekend together."

"Exactly. What we've shared has been incredible. Perfect. Let's keep it that way." She tried to plaster on another of those phony smiles that were all teeth and no heart, but her face simply wouldn't cooperate. Eyes flooding, mouth trembling, she reached up and pressed a kiss to his cheek. "Thank you again. For everything."

His arms closed around her. She felt his chest heave, his mouth rest soft against her forehead, and knew she had to escape now, or break every promise she'd made to herself not to fall apart at the last minute. "Goodbye, Domenico," she whispered, and grabbing the handle on her suitcase, turned blindly to the door.

At the last minute, he spoke again, his voice a raspy shadow of its usual self. "Don't leave, Arlene."

She didn't look back. She couldn't. "I have to."

A heartbeat passed and she heard him sigh. "Then go if you must," he said, "but do it quickly."

A blessed numbness carried her through the next several hours. After one look at her face, Gail took over the business of checking them in, finding their departure gate, and settling her in her window seat. Not until they were well out across the Atlantic, and all but the champagne from lunch had been cleared away, did she say, "Okay, what gives? We're sitting here in the lap of luxury, courtesy of your man, but there was no sign of him at the airport and you look as if you're headed to your own funeral."

"He didn't come to the airport, and he's not mine."

"You had a falling out? A conflict of schedule?"

"Neither. Our time together ended, and we've gone our separate ways."

"Temporarily."

"Permanently."

"Don't be ridiculous!" Gail snorted. "A man doesn't go to all this trouble for a woman he doesn't care about."

"In this case, he does. He'd have done the same for anybody he decided could use a little help."

"I don't call flying the pair of us Executive Class from Paris to Toronto 'a little help,' especially since he wouldn't recognize me if he fell over me on the street."

"You're my friend."

"My point exactly. This is all about his feelings for you." Gail cleared her throat. "Not that it's any of my business, but you did sleep with him, didn't you?"

Arlene turned to the window, to the bright blue arc of sky beyond. As blue as his eyes. As empty as a future without him. The feeling seeped back into her body, and the pain that came with it was ferocious. Relentless. "Yes, but it didn't mean anything."

Gail choked on her glass of champagne. "He was a dud between the sheets? I don't believe it!"

"He was perfect. He *is* perfect. To everyone. All the time. He didn't single me out for attention."

"He said nothing about seeing you again?"

"He mentioned it."

"Aha!"

"He was being polite. Chivalrous."

"So no real expression of regret? No reluctance to let you go?"

...leave if you must, but do it quickly....

"A little, perhaps."

"And when you actually walked out the door?"

She felt again the soft touch of his mouth at her brow, the deep shudder of his chest. Heard the unwonted hoarseness in his voice, the sigh he hadn't been able to suppress. "I think we both found it...difficult."

"How about heartbreaking, Arlene? Or are you so afraid of the word 'love' that you can't find room for it in your image of what this relationship's really all about?"

But men like him didn't fall for women like her. She'd have done better to lock herself in a nunnery than go to bed with him. "It can't be love," she said wearily.

"I don't know about that," Gail replied, with characteristic bluntness. "In my experience, if it walks like a duck, and it quacks like a duck, it probably is a duck! So don't be too ready to turn your back on what might be the best thing that's ever happened to you."

The trouble was, Arlene knew the difference between pity and love, and between charity and love. Neither was an acceptable substitute. "Perhaps, but I can't think about it anymore," she said, reclining her seat and tucking a pillow behind her head. "I've hardly slept, the last two nights, and nothing's making much sense right now."

Originally he'd booked through from Paris to Santiago on a commercial flight after his Sunday meetings were concluded, but the emotional turmoil of the morning left Domenico in too foul a mood to be sociable with whoever happened to be sitting next to him. His own jet would get him where he had to go, but it involved three or more refueling stops and any number of delays. He was in no mood for that, either.

"Conspicuous consumption be damned," he muttered, and chartered a Gulfstream 450, scheduled to leave Le Bourget at nine that night. He'd be served an excellent dinner, do a little work and sleep comfortably during the flight which, even allowing for one refueling stop, shouldn't take more than fifteen hours. He'd be in Santiago by nine at the latest, Chile time, ready for the start of the business day. And far enough removed from anything to do with Arlene Russell that he shouldn't have any trouble putting her out of his mind.

All things considered, he ought to be glad she'd been so ready to move on. He'd accomplished what he set out to do, and done it well. She'd made useful contacts, impressed all the right people and he could go forward with a clear conscience.

Yet all through the long flight to South America, she was there inside his head. Worse, inside his heart. Her intelligence, her smile, her laugh, her impudent little shrug, her long, lovely legs and warm body…

Let me please you, she'd begged, just the other night, as if giving herself to him so sweetly, so generously, wasn't reward enough in itself. How had it happened that she'd so thoroughly invaded that part of him no other woman had managed to touch?

Groaning inwardly, he leaned his head against the back of the seat and closed his eyes, trying to shut her out. He'd be better off with someone like Ortensia Costanza, who never in a million years could turn his life upside-down.

Cold comfort, certainly, given his present state of mind, but he wasn't so far gone that he was willing to delude himself. *We're from different worlds,* Arlene had said—or words to that effect—and he could hardly deny the truth of that.

Sardinia was a land steeped in ancient customs,

so culturally distinct from other regions of Europe that even mainland Italians felt like foreigners when they visited. But he was Sard through and through. Its emerald seas, untamed mountains and harsh sirocco winds were in his blood.

He might travel the world, own pieds-à-terre in Britain, France, the States and Australia. Yet only with the sandy clay and granite foundation of his island under his feet was he ever really at home, and he knew himself too well to think he could set up permanent residence anywhere else. But Arlene had made it clear her future was bound up in an inheritance that lay half a world away.

Even with reality staring him in the face, though, she continued to linger. *Nice legs*, he heard her whisper, when he went to taste the glass of wine the flight steward served him, an hour out of Paris. From there, it was a quantum leap of memory to *her* legs, long and luscious, wrapped around his waist, and the inarticulate little whimpers she made just before she came.

The idea of her responding to any other man like that filled him with black rage. She belonged to him.

Except, she didn't want him. And what kind of fool was he even to be thinking that four nights of unparalleled sex made for a sound and lasting relationship? He'd bedded enough women in his time to know better—more than one in Santiago where it was summertime and he could forget the chill, brisk winds of Paris, and Arlene Russell's sweet face and clear gray eyes, and warm, delicious body.

She spent her first night back in Canada at Gail's apartment, just long enough to return the things she'd borrowed and catch her breath before she boarded another jet, the next day, and headed west.

British Columbia's interior greeted her with a blast of Arctic air and snowflakes drifting down from a leaden sky. She'd phoned ahead, to alert Cal Sweeney, the caretaker, to her arrival. But her house, the first she'd ever lived in as an adult, let alone owned, was no more inviting than the weather. Gloomy and neglected, it begged for a woman's touch. Cal, though, whom she'd met only briefly the first time she'd visited, had little faith in women in general and her in particular, something he made abundantly clear, the minute he opened the front door to her.

"Reckon you'll last as long in these parts as a hothouse flower in winter," he declared sourly, eyeing the fancy suede boots and woollen cape she'd bought in Alghero, a small lifetime ago. "Well, since you're the boss now and you're here anyway, I suppose I have to let you in, though I'm danged if I know what use you'll be. Reckon old Frank lost what few marbles he had left, to be handing this place over to a city wench from down east."

"Lovely to see you again, too, Mr. Sweeney," she replied sweetly, marching past him and surveying her domain.

Like the one at Domenico's parents' home, the entrance hall was large and lofty, with a staircase rising at one side. It even had a rather grand old library table centered under a wrought-iron chandelier. But there the resemblance ended. This table was piled high with yellowed newspapers, and half the bulbs were burned out in the chandelier. She supposed she should be grateful. More reminders of Domenico she did not need. He already filled her every waking thought.

Down in the cellar, a furnace clanked and groaned, blowing blasts of hot air through the heating vents and disturbing the dust balls nestled along the baseboards, which shouldn't have come as any great surprise. The first time she'd seen the house, she'd realized it needed work. But the sun had been shining that day, and she was filled with hope and excitement. In today's dim light, it looked infinitely worse than she remembered. Grim, depressed and totally devoid of optimism, it was, she thought, right in sync with the way she felt.

As if sensing her sadness, the greyhounds loped over and pushed their cold, damp noses against her leg. Bending down, she stroked their silky heads. "What are the dogs' names again? Sable—?"

"Sam and Sadie. And I'm tellin' you now, forget any ideas you might have about getting rid of 'em. They go, I go with 'em—and, missy, you'll be up the creek without paddle if I'm not around to steer you in the right direction."

"I have no intention of getting rid of them," she informed him. "Given your attitude, though, I might decide I can do very well without you."

His faded blue eyes almost disappearing in the network of weathered wrinkles that made up his face, he inspected her at further length, then crowed with sudden laughter. "Got a real mouth on you, haven't you, missy? Maybe you're Frank's kin, after all."

A dubious and decidedly backhanded compliment at best, she thought, but sensed she'd passed some sort of test. "Thank you—I think!"

He nodded and jerked his head to where the taxi driver had left her suitcases at the foot of the steps. "I'll give you a hand carting in your bags. You want 'em in the big room facing the lake?"

"I don't think so. I'd like to take another look around first." She glanced at the drab green paint adorning the walls. As she recalled, the same uninspired color scheme pretty much ran through the whole house, and she couldn't see the point of moving into the master bedroom until she'd fixed it up to her liking. "For now, leave them in the room at the top of the stairs—unless that's where you sleep."

He let fly with another cackle. "Not likely, missy! Me and the hounds live in the old maid's suite, the other side of the kitchen. You've got this end of the house all to yourself."

He hauled her suitcases inside and started up the stairs, leaving her to rediscover the main floor. Both the large living room and formal dining room had fireplaces which probably hadn't been used in years, judging by the cobwebs festooning their tarnished brass andirons. But the tiles surrounding them were hand painted and quite lovely, as she saw when she rubbed at the dust dulling their surface. And the fir floors, though in similarly sad shape, would be gorgeous when they were cleaned up, as would the tall windows.

It had been a beautiful house once, and it could be again, given a little elbow grease and a fresh coat of paint. "Just what I need to take my mind off *him*," she murmured to the dogs, who'd followed her on her tour. If she worked outside when the weather permitted, and tackled the interior of the house when it didn't, perhaps she'd end up exhausted enough to fall into bed at night and sleep, instead of lying awake pining for a man who, despite his apparent reluctance to let her go, had done so anyway.

A big country kitchen, a small room that might serve as an office, and a powder room completed the downstairs, except for Cal Sweeney's quarters, which were quite separate, situated as they were in their own wing. Upstairs were four bedrooms and two baths. An awful lot of house for one lovesick woman, two dogs and an ill-tempered old man, but even today, the view from the windows was stunning.

The bare branches of the gnarled old fruit trees in the garden rose black against the sky. If the cold weather continued overnight, by morning the tangle of unpruned shrubs and overgrown flower beds would be hidden under a blanket of snow. A thin skin of ice covered the surface of the lake and to the west, on the far shore, a ridge of hills cast dark shadows over the landscape. On a clear day, it would look like a Christmas card. Perhaps in this quiet place, which held no memories of Domenico, she would one day find peace again, and hope, and happiness.

"I made stew," Cal announced, coming upon her toward evening, as she inspected the contents of the refrigerator. "It's not fancy, but there's enough for you, if you don't mind eating in the kitchen."

Recognizing the invitation as an overture of sorts, she accepted and sat at the table, watching as he ladled chunks of meat and vegetables onto plates, filled two bowls for the dogs, and cut thick slices of bread.

"Got this at the bakery in town," he said, rapping the loaf with the knife. "There's a decent market there, as well. You don't need to drive thirty miles to the next stop down the highway, unless you're too posh to buy from the locals."

"I'm not too posh, Cal," she told him quietly. "I'm an ordinary working individual, just like you."

"Well, you've taken on a hell of a job by coming here, missy. This property's been dying on its feet for years. I can't remember the last time we brought in a decent harvest."

"I know. And I'm counting on you to help me bring it back to life."

"Got pots of money stashed in them suitcases, have you?"

"No. But I have an apartment I'm selling, and savings bonds I can use in the meantime—even a pension fund I can access, at a pinch."

He waved his fork at her. "And what do you know about growing grapes?"

"Next to nothing," she admitted, and winced inwardly at the poignant stab of memories suddenly crowding her mind. If only there was a way to retain everything she'd learned, but erase all thought of the man who'd taught her. "How much do you know?"

"Enough."

"Then I'll learn from you."

"Reckon you don't have much choice," he grumbled, but she heard the note of respect in his voice.

"We'll start tomorrow."

"Not much you can do in this weather."

"Unless we wake up to a foot of snow, we can take a look at the fields and talk about what has to be done when spring comes."

"Not if you plan to wear them silly boots," he said. "They'll be next to useless."

"Okay, we'll begin with a trip to town. You be my guide and show me where to shop and what to buy."

He dropped his fork with a clatter and stared at her, bug-eyed. "You kidding me, missy? I don't shop for women's things."

"How about a car, then? I didn't bother with one in Toronto, but I can see I'll need one here."

"That I can do," he said, and actually smiled at her. "Maybe you'll do, too, missy, with me around to keep you in line."

And so began their unlikely friendship. Cal Sweeney was no elegant, mannerly, silver-haired Emile. He was cantankerous, rough around the edges and unabashedly outspoken. But he was on her side, and he had a soft spot for the dogs.

Would it be enough, she wondered.

At first, it seemed it would, because she refused to leave herself enough time to look at the alternatives. She outfitted herself for winter in the country, and decided buying a truck made more sense than a car.

The furniture and other belongings she'd had shipped out from Toronto finally arrived. She stowed everything in the garage until she'd cleaned up the house. For the present, she was using only one bedroom, one bathroom and the kitchen. The other rooms she put on hold.

She walked over every inch of her land, taking comfort in the knowledge that it *was* her land, despite the ragged disrepair of its trellises, its outdated irrigation system and general air of desolate abandonment. She began the backbreaking task of clearing the near acre, hoping that, when spring came, at least some of it would be ready for planting.

After observing from a distance for several days, Cal eventually joined her. "Didn't reckon you'd stick with it," he declared, at the end of the second week, when she was so stiff and sore from the arduous pace she'd set herself, she could barely walk.

"I'm not giving up," she told him, massaging her aching back. "I don't know how I'll do it, but I'm going to make a success of this vineyard or die trying,"

"And I ain't givin' up on you, missy," he said gruffly. "We're in this together."

When the snow returned at the beginning of December and put an end to working outside, she turned her attention to fixing up the house. She shoveled out years of rubbish, and scrubbed everything down until her hands were raw.

She found an old sewing machine in the attic, bought a bolt of heavy burgundy brocade at a fire sale and made drapes for all the windows. Some of the old furniture she'd inherited was good for nothing but firewood, but other pieces she brought back to life, removing years of grime with solvent, then rubbing them to a satin finish with lavender scented beeswax.

All this cost money, far more than she'd anticipated. She was depleting her savings at an alarming rate, in a driven attempt to turn her lurking, ever-present misery into joy. Sorting through the debris and neglect to find contentment, and struggling to make ends meet until her apartment sold.

The withered vines, the house, the dogs and Cal—*these* were what her life was all about now. She had to make a success of it.

She prayed to forget Domenico, but her prayers went unanswered. In response to her letter of thanks to his parents, she'd received warm replies, not just from them but from his sisters, too.

"We hoped we'd see you again before you returned home," Renata had written. "Come back again and stay longer, the next time."

But there hadn't been a word from him. No doubt he'd moved on to another needy case. Yet he was everywhere that Arlene turned: in the gravelly soil when she climbed the slope of the land; in the bare rows of the vines, and the still moonlit night. She heard his voice as she painted the old house, buffed its floors and polished its windows. She saw his face in the frozen surface of the lake, in the wind-driven clouds racing across the sky.

The worst by far, though, was when she sat in bed at night, supposedly trying to formulate a plan of action that wouldn't strip away the last of her dwindling resources, but instead recalling in vivid, tactile detail the times she'd been in bed with him. How she'd cried out his name when he brought her to orgasm. How she'd bitten her knuckles to stifle the words she'd longed to utter: *I love you!*

Long distance relationships have never appealed to me, he'd said, that last day in Paris. *Better to make a clean break now. Neither of us would be happy with an occasional weekend....*

At the time, she'd convinced herself he was right, but knew now that he'd been wrong. Anything was better than nothing—a weekend, a day, an hour. If he was to phone her…

Sam and Sadie watched her mournfully when she cried, and butted her anxiously with their soft muzzles. Cal scolded her for wearing herself to a shadow trying to restore the house.

"Rome wasn't built in a day, missy. This place's been falling apart for years, and you ain't gonna bring it back to glory overnight, no more than them withered old vines out there is gonna bear fruit next summer."

She'd given Domenico everything she was, everything she had: her body, her heart, her soul. But when their time together ended, she'd walked away and he'd let her go. Now, the only ones on earth who cared whether she lived or died were Cal and the greyhounds.

They had to be enough. They *had* to be!

But money was tight. The only offer she'd received on her apartment had fallen through when the prospective buyer had failed to qualify for a mortgage, and as the second week of December dragged to a close, she knew that her only hope of keeping her little family together left her with only one option.

CHAPTER TEN

"To SECURE our future," she'd told Cal the next day, when he'd asked where she was going, *all dressed up to the nines like some city wench.* "Break out the homemade wine. Tonight, we celebrate."

Two hours later, she drove out of town to a stretch of road that saw very little traffic. There she pulled over, switched off the engine and putting her head down on the steering wheel, she burst into tears.

Ralph McKinley, the bank manager, had refused her application for a loan. She had not, as she'd assumed, inherited her seven acres of vineyards outright. She had inherited the remaining ninety years of a ninety-nine-year lease on aboriginal land owned by the local First Nations Band. And what that meant, in terms of cold, hard cash, was that she had only her house and outbuildings to put up as collateral, which, according to McKinley, wasn't nearly enough.

According to him, the best she could hope was that a private investor would step forward and provide the financial resources she needed. "A slim chance, at best," he'd told her frankly, "and usually one that comes with a very high rate of interest, but such offers do happen occasionally if a company is looking for a tax shelter."

How had things come to such a pass? she wondered miserably. Three months ago, her life had been in perfect, albeit unexciting order. Now it was in a tailspin. Her savings were almost all gone, the money she hoped to make on the sale of her apartment hadn't yet materialized and she was worried sick, stressed out, heartbroken and completely exhausted. And if all that wasn't enough, Christmas lay just around the corner and it promised to be the bleakest she'd ever known—which, given her unhappy childhood, was saying a lot.

She had no one to blame but herself for her sorry situation. She'd rushed into accepting a legacy without reading the fine print in her great-uncle's will, and she'd rushed into an affair with a charismatic stranger without calculating the emotional price she'd have to pay. And the result was a meltdown of gigantic proportion, on a strip of deserted road in a remote corner of British Columbia held in the iron grip of winter.

"You're looking a bit green around the gills,

missy," Cal announced, when she finally pulled herself together enough to make it home. "The future ain't looking as bright you thought it was, is it?"

Too worn down to put a brave face on the situation, she said, "I tried to borrow money from the bank, but they turned me down, and if my apartment doesn't sell soon, Cal, I don't know how I can keep this place going."

"What do you mean, 'you?' We're in this together, Arlene, and I've got a few dollars stashed away that you can have."

He almost never called her "Arlene." That he did so now, and with such rough affection, tipped her over the edge into another flood of tears. "I can't take your money," she wailed.

"Don't see why not. I've got no use for it," he said, practically pushing her into the living room where a fire blazed in the hearth. "As for that place you've got down east, somebody'll buy it, sooner or later, so stop your bawling. It's upsetting our dogs."

"Oh, Cal!" She smeared her hands over her face and managed a watery smile. "How will I ever repay you for sticking by me through all this?"

"I'll tell you how. Get yourself to the clinic in town and tell that half-assed young sprig that calls himself a doctor to give you the once-over. You're not the weepy kind, missy. It takes more than a bit of a setback to make you cry. Wouldn't surprise me if your battery's low, what with the way you've been knocking yourself out with this house, and you need a pick-me-up of some sort."

"You might be right," she admitted. "I *have* been feeling a bit run-down, lately. I'll book an appointment for next week."

"Right." He hooked his thumbs in his belt and looked around the room. "Now, where do you want the Christmas tree?"

"I wasn't planning on having one," she said, jarred out of her self-pity by the sudden change of subject.

"Too damn bad. I went out and cut one while you were gone this morning. So make up your mind where it goes, or I'll do it for you."

"I…suppose in the corner between the windows."

"Glad you think so because that's where it's going anyway. I'll get started on it while you make us something to eat. I'm so hungry, my stomach's beginning to think my throat's been cut."

At that she actually managed a laugh. "Let me change out of this suit," she said, heading for the stairs, "then I'll fix us some soup and a sandwich. But about the tree, Cal, you know we don't have any decorations or lights for it?"

"That don't matter as long as it smells right.

Anyhow, the idea's what counts. Families put up Christmas trees, it's as simple as that."

He'd never know how his words affected her; how they lifted her spirits. She'd envied other people all her life for the families they took for granted, and learned to guard her heart against the hurt. But Domenico had managed to steal it in a matter of weeks—of days, even. He'd made her aware of all she'd missed, not just passion on a grand scale, but the warmth of belonging.

Well now, after nearly thirty years, she had Cal and she had the greyhounds. Not much by most people's standards, probably, but they gave her a sense of belonging she'd never before known. Even though the man she missed with an ache that never went away, wasn't part of the package, they helped make the pain just a little more bearable.

She set up an appointment at the clinic for the following Monday afternoon. Aware that Christmas was just three days away and she'd done nothing to make it special, she decided to dip into her meager savings and go shopping beforehand.

She was ready to leave the house just after eleven, when Ralph McKinley phoned and asked her to stop by his office. Frowning, she said, "I've got some time today, if that's convenient, but I hope it's not more bad news. I'm not overdrawn on my account, am I?"

"No, no," he said, sounding positively festive. "Nothing like that. What time's good for you?"

"I can be there in half an hour."

"Fine," he said. "See you then. Oh, and Ms. Russell? I think you're going to be very pleased with my news."

Had Great-Uncle Frank left a safe-deposit box full of hundred-dollar bills no one had remembered to tell her about? she wondered, slowing down at the intersection to Main Street and pulling into a parking slot right outside the bank.

"A little brisk out, isn't it?" Ralph McKinley remarked jovially, greeting her at the door and ushering her into his office. "May I get my assistant to bring you coffee to warm you up, Ms. Russell?"

"No, thank you," she said. She was off coffee, lately. Not only that, this office held no fond memories for her and she wasn't sure the butter-flies in her stomach could tolerate extra company. Despite his earlier reassurances, she was as nervous now as she had been the first time she sat across the desk from him.

"Then I'll get straight to the point. You might recall, when you were here last, my mentioning that certain wealthy individuals occasionally choose to back ventures that fall outside the boundaries set by official lending institutions such as ours."

"Yes," she said, hard-pressed not to tell him to forget the jargon and cut to the chase. "Are you saying someone has expressed an interest in my situation?"

"In fact, yes." He pushed a single sheet of paper across the desk. "The fine print is all here, but what it essentially boils down to is that a private party has offered to finance the restoration of your vineyard far beyond anything the bank could offer, even if it were in a position to lend you the money you need."

"You also told me that this kind of offer comes at a much higher cost than that charged by the bank."

"Not in this case, as it happens. The agreement calls for you to do the work, and the investor to provide the funding, in effect becoming a silent partner."

"Who'll take my property if I default on repayment."

"No. The terms of the agreement stipulate two conditions only—an equal share of future profits, and first option to buy out your half of the business at fair market value, should you decide to sell."

"Why would anyone want it, if the land isn't part of the deal?"

"Because your lease is good for another ninety

years. With the right backing and proper management, there's a fortune to be made in a tenth of that time. From a purely practical standpoint, the return on a fifty percent share of profits over the long-term far outstrips what an investor could normally expect to make on a standard loan, even allowing for a higher than normal interest rate."

"It sounds too good to be true. Who is this angel of mercy?"

"No name that would mean anything to you. It's a numbered company, WMS830090. But I can tell you that the offer is entirely legitimate and aboveboard. Take a moment to look over the contract, Ms. Russell. It's very straightforward and will, I think, put your mind at ease. Then, if you're satisfied with what you see and are agreeable, I'll witness your signature and the money will be transferred into your account immediately."

"And if I have questions?"

"I'm authorized to answer them. Now if you'll excuse me, I need to have a word with one of my tellers."

Left alone, Arlene took a deep breath and tried to control her trembling hands. If this was a genuine offer, it was also a godsend. But it was Christmas, the season of miracles, and maybe she should be thankful one had come her way, instead of sniffing around like a suspicious bloodhound.

But, *Don't be hasty this time,* her common sense cautioned. *Read every word twice—on the lines and between them, too.* As contracts went, this one might be simple as ABC, but she'd sign nothing until a lawyer had gone over it with a fine-tooth comb.

"I'll give Greg Lawson a call," McKinley offered, when she told him her decision. "His office is just across the street. You could go over there right away, if he's free."

As it happened, the lawyer was just leaving for lunch and, agreeing to stop by the bank on his way out, showed up within minutes. "I have no problem advising you to accept any of this, Arlene," he said, after examining the document thoroughly. "My only question is, who signs on behalf of the investor company?"

"I do," Ralph McKinley said. "I have power of attorney to represent the client."

The lawyer shrugged. "Then grab a pen and Merry Christmas, Arlene!"

People really couldn't walk on air. They put one foot in front of the other and very carefully made their way along the icy sidewalk. But Arlene's spirits soared sky high as she headed home just after four o'clock, with a clean bill of health and a truck full of goodies.

"You had a complete physical less than six months ago, so I don't see the need for another at this time," the doctor had said, after checking her heart, her lungs and her blood pressure. "I'll send blood samples to the lab, just to be on the safe side, but as far as I can tell, there's not much wrong with you that a restful, relaxed Christmas won't fix."

From there, she'd driven to the shopping mall in another, larger town, several miles farther down the highway. Tonight, there'd be wrapped gifts for Cal and the greyhounds, under a tree decorated with strings of colored lights and shiny glass balls.

That evening, when he came in from stacking more firewood on the back porch, she had Cal's favorite dinner waiting: roast prime rib of beef, mashed potatoes, carrots and gravy, and a bottle of good red wine, with hot apple pie and ice cream for dessert. Plain, honest food, just like him, served in the dining room instead of the kitchen, with candles on the table, and festive paper napkins.

"Pretty fancy," he declared, eyeing his plate. "We come into money, did we?"

"As a matter of fact, we did," she replied, and told him about her meeting at the bank.

"Something fishy about this deal, if you ask me," he rumbled. "Folk don't give somethin' without expecting something in return—especially not rich folk! That's how they made their money in the first place. Mark my words, missy, there's a catch somewhere. You just ain't bumped into it yet."

"If there is, it sneaked past a bank manager and a lawyer. Both Ralph McKinley and Greg Lawson gave their stamp of approval."

"McKinley's a sharp cookie," he admitted grudgingly. "Not much gets by him. And young Lawson's not so bad, either, considerin' he a lawyer."

"Exactly! And it's not as if I've signed away my inheritance."

"You've given some stranger first dibs at buying this place if you decide to sell," he said darkly.

"I have no intention of selling, if that's what's worrying you." She looked around at the walls newly painted a soft butter-cream; at the sparkling moldings, the gleaming floor. Logs crackled in the fireplace, while outside, fat snowflakes drifted down and batted against the windows like blind white moths. Across the hall, the lights from the Christmas tree threw muted shades of color across the living room. "I love this place, Cal. It's become my home—and you're my family."

He cleared his throat and made a big production of piling potatoes on his fork. "Some family!" he muttered hoarsely. "A wench like you should have a husband and kids, not be making do with a couple of aging dogs and an old fart like me."

"Not even if I happen to be rather fond of aging dogs and old farts?"

He let out one of his famous cackles. "Watch your mouth, missy, unless you want it washed out with soap."

Smiling, she sat in silence a while, more at peace than she'd been in weeks. She didn't delude herself. She knew the road ahead would be hard, that money alone wasn't enough to bring her vineyard back to life; that it required dedication and commitment and patience.

She knew, too, that the perennial ache of missing Domenico would continue to haunt her in the middle of the night, or make a sneak attack during the day, and that when it did, the pain it brought would leave her breathless. Which was why she was so grateful for times like this, when contentment reigned supreme, even if it was only for a little while.

"We've never talked about this before, Cal," she said, after the meal was cleared away and they sat by the fire in the living room, with the dogs snoozing at their feet, "but how did this place fall into such disrepair?"

"Liquor," he said bluntly. "Frank always liked his booze, but he really started hitting the bottle about seven years back, when we lost most of the harvest two seasons in a row. Drank himself to death in the end. I love everything to do with growin' wine grapes, and tried to keep things going, but it's more than a one-man job and I ain't as young as I used to be. You want to make a go of it here, Arlene, you're gonna have to hire extra labor, come spring."

"I'll be relying on you to do that. As far as I'm concerned, you're the man in charge of the vineyard and what you say, goes."

He shuffled to his feet. "Reckon I can live with that, missy," he said. "You okay here by yourself for a spell?"

"Of course. It's been a long day, so I'm going to put my feet up and enjoy the fire and the Christmas tree, and maybe watch a little TV."

"Then I'll throw a couple more logs on the fire, and take the dogs for a run before I turn in myself."

After he'd gone, she went upstairs, took a quick shower and put on a long white nightgown embroidered with rosebuds and forget-me-nots, her warm rose-pink chenille dressing gown and matching slippers. So what if she looked like somebody's granny? It wasn't as if she was expecting company.

Scooping up the contract she'd left on the hall table, she returned to the living room and had just settled down in her favorite armchair when the doorbell rang.

Thinking Cal must have accidentally locked himself out at the back, she trudged through the hall and opened the front door.

Sure enough, Cal stood there with the dogs, but they weren't alone. "Caught this guy snooping around the place," he said. "Drivin' the same car as I saw creeping around here yesterday like a fox circling the henhouse. Claims you know him. That so?"

"Yes, I know him," she said dully. And she knew, too, in a flash of insight as blinding as it was devastating, exactly who her anonymous benefactor was.

"Arlene," Domenico said, wrapping her in the unforgettable, sexy timbre of his voice. "It's wonderful to see you again. May I come in?"

CHAPTER ELEVEN

FROM her expression, he was obviously about as welcome as the bubonic plague, and given the way she'd walked away from him in Paris, he supposed he shouldn't have expected anything else. But she'd haunted him for weeks now, and he was tired of being on the losing end of a battle he hadn't a hope of winning. Like it or not, she was in his blood. The time had come to win her over, or exorcise her from his mind *and* his heart, once and for all.

"May I come in?" he asked again, locking gazes with her.

She gave the merest nod and moved well back, as if afraid that if he touched her, he might contaminate her. She'd lost weight, he noticed. Although the loose robe she wore camouflaged her body, the hollows beneath her cheekbones were more pronounced, her jaw more sharply defined. She looked drained, exhausted, and he had an overpowering impulse to gather her in his arms and never let her go.

Why hadn't she taken better care of herself? And why had he waited so long to come to her rescue?

Stamping the snow from his shoes, he stepped inside.

The old man slammed the door shut. "You want me to stick around, missy?" he asked, fixing Domenico in an evil glare.

"It's not necessary," she said. "Our visitor won't be staying long."

"I'll be in the kitchen, if you change your mind."

"Thanks, Cal."

She waited until he'd disappeared before turning her attention to Domenico again. "Why are you here?"

"Because I couldn't stay away."

She curled her lip. "Of course not. What satisfaction is there in conferring favors on someone, if you're not on hand to wallow in their gratitude? The only surprise is that you waited this long to show up."

He'd bent down to stroke the dogs who were winding around his legs, begging for affection, but at her words, he abruptly straightened again. *"What?"*

"Oh, please!" she said scornfully, heading for a room to the right of the front door. "I know you're my anonymous investor, Domenico. The pity of it is that I didn't figure it out sooner. It's not as if your friend Ortensia didn't warn me."

He followed her and found himself in a handsome salon illuminated only by the lights on a fragrant Christmas tree and the flames in the tiled hearth leaping up the chimney. "What has Ortensia Costanza to do with any of this?"

"She told me you coveted my land. I didn't believe her." Her lovely mouth curved in a bitter smile. "Silly me! I should have remembered you were the one who told me you don't let anything stand in the way of your going after the things you want."

"Did it ever occur to you that I might want you?"

"You had me, Domenico. In Paris."

A flicker of anger ruffled his composure. "Disdain me if you must, Arlene, but do not try to cheapen what we shared in Paris. I will not allow it."

"And I will not allow you to manipulate me. I am not a plaything you may pick up or leave at whim."

She darted to a table next to an armchair by the fire, grabbed what he at once recognized as the contract he'd had drawn up, and flung it at him. Catching it in one hand, he said, "I've never treated you as such. Where you're concerned, I have always acted in good faith."

"You have tried to buy me, and I'm not for sale."

"I have tried to help you because I care about you."

"I don't want you to *care* about me, and I don't need your help. So if you came all the way from Sardinia to dig me out of the hole you think I'm in, you've wasted your time."

"I was already in North America, and decided to stop by to see you, on my way home."

She shot him a look of pure disbelief. "Where in North America?"

"My alma mater in Fresno, California."

"California?" She gave a hoot of laughter but it was belied by the desolation in her gray eyes. "I suggest you took a wrong turn somewhere south of the border!"

He unbuttoned his overcoat. "That's one of the perks of owning my own jet, Arlene," he drawled. "Within reason, I get to choose in which direction it flies and where it lands. In this case, I chose here, because from everything I've heard—"

"What have you heard?" she flared. "Who's been talking about me behind my back? If it was Ralph McKinley at the bank—"

"It wasn't Ralph McKinley," he said. "*Dio,* Arlene, I've got business contacts all over the world, including this little corner of it. A couple of phone calls were enough to confirm what I'd suspected all along. You've inherited serious trouble with this property and need a hefty infusion of cash to get you out of it."

"So you rushed in to save the day?" She shot the question at him, loaded with sarcasm.

Steeling himself to patience, he said, "Somebody had to, and I didn't see anyone else volunteering for the job. I wasn't about to stand idly by and do nothing. That's not how I operate, Arlene."

"I know exactly how you operate," she said, her eyes suddenly bright with tears. "You use money to buy whatever you want, whether it happens to be things or people. You bought a château in France because, to quote you, it took your fancy. Then you bought a family to run it for you. You don't live there, so to give the staff something to do besides rattle around in a place large enough to be a hotel, you sponsor underprivileged children to spend their summers there."

"Not just their summers," he interrupted curtly. "They come at Christmas and Easter, too. They fill the rooms with their laughter, and they spill milk and cookie crumbs on the furniture. They race over the grounds, sail little wooden boats on the lake, climb trees and learn to swim in the pool. If you're going to run an inventory of my perceived failings, at least do me the courtesy of getting all the facts before you condemn me."

She grimaced, disgust plain on her face. "The

point is, you're a collector, Domenico, and you particularly like collecting needy people because it makes you feel good. And if the flavor of the month happens also to hold a lease on a prime chunk of land, well, why not acquire the rights to that, too, while you're at it? Not because it once belonged to royalty like your château. Not because its vineyards are flourishing. Not for any reason at all but because you *fancy* it."

Breasts heaving, she stopped just long enough to draw in an irate breath before firing a last shot. "But I'll see you in hell before I let you have it!"

Astounded by her outburst, he shook his head. "Do you hear yourself, woman? To suggest I'm after your land is ludicrous. Tell me what possible use I have for seven paltry acres when I have hundreds at my disposal all over the world, and every one of them doing what yours are not—namely producing quality wine grapes."

"Exactly!" she burst out, the tears slipping down her cheeks. "You have no use for them at all. You're not driven by *need*. You just enjoy *managing* people's lives. Well, you're not managing mine, so take your money and take yourself out of here!"

Her distress moved him more than he cared to admit. He had to hold himself back from cradling her body next to his and kissing away her anger, her suspicions and everything else that troubled her, along with her tears. But shocked by her lack of trust in his motives, he remained motionless. "If that's how you see me—as some paternalistic figure using you to boost his own ego—then there's nothing more to be said."

"Finally we agree on something!"

"Except this." He pulled his own copy of the contract from the inside pocket of his overcoat and, together with hers, ripped the papers in half and flung them on the fire. "There! You're off the hook. No silent partner trying to control your fate. No first option clause to buy you out if you ever decide to sell. Your precious land is safe, and so are you. I'm out of your life, as of now."

"Good!" she quavered. "Take your money with you when you go."

"I'm afraid I can no longer do that. It's deposited to your account and even I, world-class manipulator that I am, can't access it."

"Well, I certainly don't want it."

"Then give it to someone who does, burn it, do what the devil you like with it." He swept his glance over the aging dogs snoozing by the fire; over the elderly caretaker who, obviously having heard the raised voices, had reappeared and stood now in the doorway, watching the final act of a fiasco the old Domenico would never have allowed to take place. "But if I had others depending on me, as you do, I'd put my pride aside and think about what's best for them before I threw away the chance to make their days more comfortable."

She started to reply, but choked on the words and buried her face in hands no longer smooth and white, but red and chapped, with the nails clipped short. A working woman's hands which it pained him to see.

Finally, in a muffled voice, she said, "Why did you have to come back into my life? Why couldn't you just leave me well enough alone?"

"It's called taking care of the people you love, Arlene, whether or not they care enough to love you back," he said, the words torn so harshly from him that his throat burned. "And if that offends your sensibilities, as well as my many other transgressions, then sue me!"

The force with which he slammed the front door as he stormed out made the dogs jump and the whole house shudder. "Pleased with yourself, are you?" Cal inquired calmly, into the ensuing silence.

Arlene lifted her head and looked at him through streaming eyes. "Don't tell me you're on his side," she wailed.

"Can't say as I see he's done anythin' so

wrong—except take a load of abuse from you, that is. You pushed that man's patience too far, missy. I'm surprised he didn't walk out on you sooner. Reckon he's just a fool for love under them slick city duds he wears."

"He only said that to justify his actions. He doesn't really love me."

"Gave a dang good imitation of it then, is all I've got to say. In his place, I'd've hightailed it outta here the minute you got on your high horse and started accusing him of being the devil bent on making your life a misery. Which when I come to think of it, don't make much sense, seein' as how, most of the time, you've been plagued with misery anyway, mooning around the place like a lost lamb practically from the day you got here."

He crossed to the hearth and threw another log on the fire. "Reckon I know why now. What beats me is you lettin' him get away when it's as plain as the noses on them greyhounds that he's the man you want. But then, I never did pretend to understand what makes a woman tick. Saved myself a load of grief by never trying, too."

Taken aback by his words, she plucked a tissue from her pocket and mopped her eyes, then paced to the window and stared out at the thickly falling snow. The roads would be treacherous, especially out here in the country. "He's not used to weather like this," she said quietly. "I hope he drives carefully."

"He don't strike me as the type to let a bit of weather get the better of him."

"Out here, he might. I don't think it ever snows in Sardinia—at least, not the part where he lives. What if he has an accident, Cal?"

Anxiety nibbled at her, eroding her indignation. She'd said harsh, unforgivable things. Things meant to wound, to inflame. She'd stirred the man she loved more than life to an anger even greater than her own. His mouth, which once had seduced her with its heat, had grown hard and cold; his eyes, stony. He'd driven away in a rage.

Just two days earlier, a stranger traveling through the area had rounded a curve in the road too fast and ended up lying injured and half-frozen in the ditch, before someone came along and found him.

If Domenico had an accident, it would be her fault. How would she live with herself then, knowing she'd acted not out of righteous indignation at all, but out of irrational disappointment that, despite everything he'd been willing to give, for her it still hadn't been enough?

She clutched the collar of her dressing gown tight around her neck, as if by doing so, she could chase away the cold finger of dread stealing up her spine. Domenico Silvaggio d'Avalos was impossible. Controlling. Devious.

And if anything happened to him, she'd die.

Why had she sent him away, when what she most wanted was to run into his arms and beg him to forget everything she'd said, that last day in Paris? He'd hinted then that he didn't want their relationship to end, but even though he'd accepted her rejection gracefully enough at the time, she realized now that he'd never really given up on her.

If all he'd wanted was to be her benefactor, he could have arranged it from anywhere in the world. He didn't have to detour through Canada from California on his way back to Sardinia. He didn't have to risk his life driving on snow-clogged, unfamiliar roads.

"We miss you," Renata had written in her Christmas card. "*All* of us."

Belatedly Arlene recognized the message for what it truly implied.

A blast of cold air snaked around Arlene's ankles. The dogs stirred, stretched and wagged their tails. Cal must have opened the door to let them out for a last run before turning in.

"If he really loved me," Arlene said, "why couldn't he just say so, Cal, instead of trying to buy me off?"

"Because you're right," a deep, familiar,

beloved voice replied. "I *am* very good at managing other people's lives—and just plain lousy at managing my own."

She spun around, her heart in her throat. He filled the doorway to the living room. Snowflakes glinted in his black hair, sprinkled his broad, black-clad shoulders. The light of battle shone in his eyes. He looked formidable. Dangerous.

"You came back!" she whispered.

"Just as well," Cal drawled. "Saves me having to go out looking for him." He squinted at them from beneath his bushy gray brows and brushed one hand against the other. "Reckon I'd better take the dogs and make myself scarce, five being a crowd and all that. The rest is up to the two of you."

Desperate to fill the silence he left behind, Arlene said, "It's a good thing you turned back. It really isn't a good night to be on the road. I have four bedrooms, not counting Cal's, so there's plenty of room for you to stay over, and—"

"I didn't come back because of the weather, Arlene."

She hardly dared phrase the question. "Why did you, then?"

"The same reason I gave, the last time you asked. Because I can't stay away, and heaven knows I've tried. When it came to recognizing what I needed to give my life true meaning, my fabled objectivity let me down badly."

He stepped closer. Trapped her against the window. Tilted her chin with his thumb so that she had to meet his gaze. "In the last two months, I've traveled to three continents and more than five countries, and you've followed me to every one. I'm here now because I've finally accepted that you're with me, no matter how far or fast I run. I can't live without you, Arlene. So unless you tell me to my face that you don't want me, ever, for any reason at all, I'm here to stay—and not in a guest bedroom, either!"

She stared at him, drowning in his summer-blue eyes. She'd been frozen inside. Gripped by hopelessness and fear. But with every word, every glance, every touch, he thawed a little more of the ice encasing her.

"Well?" he murmured. "What's your answer, *cara mia*? Am I wasting my time and yours, or do you care for me at least a little?"

"You know I do," she said on a trembling sigh.

"Enough to make a life with me?"

"How can I? Your home is in Sardinia."

"Yours could be, too." He closed in on her. Touched her jaw, traced a path over her throat, his fingers cool and sure.

"I can't just walk away from here," she protested. "When I accepted my inheritance, I made a commitment, to Cal and to the dogs. That might sound odd to you, but—"

"It sounds like the woman I know," he said. "The one who stands by her promises and who taught me that sharing everything but his heart makes a pauper of a man."

"What are you saying?" she breathed, afraid to read more into his words than he meant.

"That I'm not asking you to break your word, or to give up this place. I understand how much it means to you."

"Not just to me. It's the only home Cal knows. He loves it here. He understands the land, and knows more about growing grapes here than I ever will. It's not his fault everything's so run-down. He wants nothing more than to see the vineyard brought back to how it used to be, before my great-uncle let it slip away, but he's too old to take on the job by himself."

"We'll find him the help he needs. It can be done, *tesoro*. We can spend part of the year here, if that's what you want. I see how beautiful your country is, and I understand the roots we all have for our native land. But I meant it when I said that long distance relationships don't work for me. I need you by my side, Arlene, wherever home happens to be."

Take what he's offering and make it be enough, because a little with him is better than nothing at all. "As what?" she said, clinging by a thread to the edge of the precipice of reason. Desperately wanting to fling herself over and listen only to the urgent pleading of her heart.

"As my wife, of course!"

"Why?"

"*Dio!* That question again! Why do you think?"

"If I knew, I wouldn't ask."

"I love you. I already told you that."

"Not really. You threw the words at me, a little while ago, but they sounded more like a curse than a blessing."

"Then let me say them again now. *I love you!* I know that's not a magic formula, that there are problems we have to iron out. And I'd take them all away, if I could—"

She placed her hand against his mouth, hushing him. "No, Domenico! That's how we went off track in the first place. I'm not a child. You don't have to shield me from reality. Life comes with problems. That's just the way it is. But a couple learns to solve them together."

He smiled and slid his hand around her neck. "That poses some very interesting possibilities," he said, inching his mouth closer to hers.

She pulled back, knowing that if he kissed her,

she'd agree to anything. "You make it all sound so simple, and it's not."

"Yes, it is," he said flatly. "The lesson I've learned is that finding the right one to love is difficult. The rest is very simple indeed." He drew her close a second time. "Must I beg?" he whispered against her hair. "Is it not enough that I offer you all that I am? That what I most want in this world is to make you happy? Can you not understand how it destroys me that you keep me at such a distance, that you refuse to let me show you, in every way, how much I treasure you?"

"Don't!" she begged, the last of her resistance washed away in a flood of scalding tears. "Please, please don't talk like that! You make me so ashamed."

"Of what? Your moral integrity? Your loyalty to those relying on you? Arlene, *mia innamorata*, these are among the reasons I fell in love with you. You are the woman I've been searching for almost half my life. Don't ask me to let you go, now that I've found you. Make my life complete. Say you'll marry me."

"Yes," she said, the last shard of ice in her heart melting under the impassioned heat of his gaze. "Oh, yes please!"

CHAPTER TWELVE

THE pain of remembering those Paris nights had been so acute that she'd willed them to die. Gradually, painstakingly, she'd buried them under the cumbersome, everyday concerns needing her attention at her new home, even likening the pang of regret that sometimes attacked, to the ghost of an amputated limb seeking to reconnect itself to its host. She'd told herself that what she'd had with Domenico was over. Nothing could bring it back again.

How quickly he taught her the error of her beliefs! In the shadowed warmth of her bedroom, with only the snowflakes nudging at the window to witness the miracle, he sealed their reconciliation, reacquainting himself with her body, and stoking the embers of buried desire with such finesse that they roared back to new life, all the wilder for their enforced hibernation.

Not an inch of her escaped his attention. "I have

missed your silken skin, your scent," he murmured, and pinning her hands above her head, took first one, then the other nipple in his mouth.

Sensation streaked through her, wild and hot; lightning that ignited every cell in her body and left her throbbing and pooling in liquid fire. "Please, Domenico," she moaned, reaching for him. "Don't make me wait…it's been so long… please…!"

He was big and hard and ready. But he would not let his hunger dominate. "I have missed how you taste," he whispered. "The memory has haunted me through every long night, and I have woken up starving for you." And running his palms down her flanks, he buried his face between her thighs. Stroked his tongue over her slick and eager flesh.

It was more torture, more ecstasy than she could withstand. Lacking his self-discipline, she exploded in a million dazzling sparks that left her begging him please, please, to fill the terrible void she'd lived with for so long.

He entered her with an urgency that belied his formidable control. Thrust himself so deep that he touched her soul. "I have dreamed of the way you sigh, as you do now, to let me know I please you," he rasped at her ear. "And I have longed to feel you close around me and drain me of my strength…" He faltered, drew in a deep, agonized breath. "As you are about to do now…Arlene, *mia innamorata…*!"

He tensed, shuddered and spilled hot and free inside her. Caught in his frenzied rhythm, she climaxed again, her flesh contracting around his so fiercely that he groaned aloud with pleasure.

It should have been enough to satisfy them, but it wasn't.

. Insatiable, inexhaustible, thrilling, the passion swept them through the quiet hours of the night until, with dawn still too distant to touch the horizon, she finally slept in his arms again, truly at peace for the first time in months.

Cal had the fire blazing in the dining room and the table laid for three when she and Domenico came downstairs, the next morning. "Reckon I don't need to ask if you got any rest last night," he commented snidely, dishing out crisp bacon and farm fresh eggs. "The pair of you look plumb wore out."

Arlene blushed, but Domenico laughed out loud. "I like a man who doesn't mince his words. In the absence of her biological father, should I ask you for your blessing, Cal? Arlene has agreed to become my wife."

"Figured somethin' of the sort must've happened. Ain't never seen her so chipper and rosy," he said gruffly. "You aim to treat her right, do you?"

"In every way, every day."

"Glad to hear it. Wouldn't want to have to take you out behind the woodshed and lay a lickin' on you."

Since Domenico stood at least six inches taller, the odds of Cal's being able to carry out his threat were about as slim as his ever needing to try, Arlene thought, burying a smile. Yet despite his apparent satisfaction with the way things had turned out, something wasn't quite right with her old friend.

"So when's the wedding?" he inquired, concentrating on his eggs.

"We haven't set a firm date," she said, "but we're thinking early in the new year."

"Reckon you'll soon be gone from here, then. Ain't no reason for you to hang around a dump like this."

"It's not a dump!" she exclaimed. "It's just…a little tired."

But Domenico, picking up on the real problem, said, "My home's in Sardinia, Cal, and yes, we'll live there some of the time, but this is Arlene's home and marrying me doesn't mean she has to give it up."

"We've talked about it, and we're hoping you'll take charge of things here when we're away," Arlene added.

"We understand you'll need help getting the land back into shape, and exactly who you hire is your choice," Domenico continued, "but you're experienced enough to know you're facing a mammoth task if you want to plant in the spring."

"And since you can't be in two places at once, we think it might be a good idea if you hire someone to take care of the household chores." Arlene looked at him questioningly. "A couple, perhaps? A woman who'll do the cooking and cleaning, and a man to tend the garden in summer, shovel snow and chop wood in winter. That kind of thing."

"I'm pretty set in my ways. Don't know as I'd want strangers underfoot all the time." Cal scratched his chin thoughtfully. "I could ask my sister, though. She still lives on the Niagara Peninsula where we grew up, but she's a widow and it's been pretty lonely for her, the last few years, seein' as she never had kids and there's no one left in the family but me."

"Do you think she'd move out here?"

"Don't see why not. Ain't nothin' keeping her there. And it'd be a shame to let the house go, after all the work you've done to make it look nice."

"We'd cover the cost of the move, of course," Domenico said, "and pay her a decent salary, just as we will you."

Cal shuffled uncomfortably in his seat. "It ain't

got nothing to do with money. That's not why I stuck around here all this time."

"I know that," Domenico said, "But a man deserves recognition for his loyalty, and Arlene is trusting you to look after her interests while she's away."

"But you're more than an employee to me, Cal," Arlene was quick to add. "You're my family, and that brings me to something else I wanted to ask you. Will you walk me down the aisle on my wedding day?"

He stared at her a moment. "You don't want me, missy. I'm not posh like you. Never have been, never will be."

"It's you or nobody—and I'm going to need a strong arm to lean on."

He pulled a red checkered handkerchief out of his jeans pocket and blew his nose. "You'll be wantin' them dogs to be bridesmaids, next."

"That hadn't occurred to me," she said, laughing. "But now that you mention it…! So what do you say, Cal? Can I count on you to be there for me?"

"Have I ever let you down?"

"Not once. I'd never have made it this far, if it hadn't been for you."

"Do I have to wear a monkey suit?"

"If I do, you do," Domenico said, with a grin.

"Where's this shindig taking place?"

Arlene was about to say they hadn't decided, but Domenico jumped in before she could speak. "Here. A bride should always be married from her own home."

"Goin' to be a pretty small wedding, then. She don't know anybody in these parts, except me."

"Well, we haven't drawn up a guest list, but my family will certainly attend, and there were twenty-three of them at the last count, although it'll probably be twenty-four by the new year."

"Spend a lot of time making babies, do they?"

"Among other things, yes."

"You plan on doing the same?"

Domenico looked at her, his glance so warm and intimate that she blushed again. "As many as Arlene wants."

"At least two," she said. "As for guests, I *do* have friends, Cal. They just happen to live too far away to visit, but I'm sure they'll come for my wedding. I hope your sister will, too. In fact, why don't you phone her this morning and sound her out on the idea of moving here?"

"Invite her for Christmas," Domenico suggested. "Give her the chance to look around the place and see what she'd be letting herself in for."

Arlene shook her head. "It's December 23. She'll never get a flight at such short notice."

"My jet's sitting on the runway, not forty kilometers away, *cara*. My pilot will have her here in time for Christmas Eve, if she chooses."

"But won't you be using the jet yourself?"

"Today. For a little while."

"More than just a little while, surely?" she said, stifling the disappointment welling up at the thought of his leaving again so soon. "It's a long way from here to Sardinia."

He raised her hand to his lips. "Who said anything about Sardinia? I'm spending Christmas with you, my love. And if it weren't that they've already made plans, I'd have my family join us. They're not used to this kind of weather, and the children would so much enjoy the snow. But there's always next year." He turned again to Cal. "Make that phone call, Cal."

"Thank you, Domenico," Arlene murmured, after Cal left the room. "I hadn't realized the impact our news would have on him—that he'd feel so...displaced. Thank you for putting his mind at ease."

"He's a good man, and I'll always be grateful to him for being here when you needed him." He pushed back his chair and dropped a kiss on her mouth. "Much though I'd rather spend the rest of the morning with you, I have to head out to the airport to take care of a little business, but I should be back no later than two or three o'clock."

"Drive carefully."

"Always," he said, and kissed her again. "I have far too much to lose, to do otherwise."

During the hours he was gone, Arlene first phoned Gail with her news and asked her to be her maid of honor, to which her friend gleefully agreed. Then, with Cal's sister, Thelma, having reluctantly agreed to spend the holiday with them, but only after much persuasion and her insistence on supplying homemade plum pudding, fruitcake and shortbread, Arlene made a run into town.

Overnight, her solitary Christmas for two had doubled to a festive four, and the roasting chicken she'd originally planned to serve wouldn't be enough. She stocked up on steaks for that night's dinner, as well as a ham, a turkey and a few other essentials to see them through the next few days.

Then, with time still hanging heavy on her hands, she went in search of a gift for her guests. She bought a lambswool scarf and bath oil for Thelma, but finding something for Domenico, the man who had everything, proved more difficult. Finally, she settled on a pair of fur-lined leather gloves, and promised herself she'd do better next year.

After lunch, she prepared a guest room for Thelma, making up the bed with freshly ironed sheets, and leaving a couple of magazines on the night table. She hung thick towels in the second bathroom, and put a basket of toiletries on the vanity.

When two o'clock came and still no sign of Domenico, she kept anxiety at bay by baking an apple pie, and preparing stuffed mushrooms and a salad to go with the steaks. She polished a pair of glass candlesticks until they sparkled like crystal, and centered them on the dining table with white candles and the scarlet poinsettia she'd bought in town.

At three-thirty, Domenico finally returned. "I was worried," she said, flying into his arms. "I thought you'd changed your mind about coming back."

"Not a chance," he assured her. "No matter where you happen to be, *tesoro*, I will always find my way back to you. Now put on a warm jacket and a pair of winter boots, and show me your garden. It is a picture such as I'm not accustomed to seeing."

They took the dogs and walked down by the lake. The air was crisp and scented with woodsmoke; a Christmas card scene, with the water frozen to a sheen, the sky a pale, cloudless winter blue and the trees draped in snow.

"I'll miss them," Arlene said, watching as Sam and Sadie raced along the shore, sleek and swift under their faded plaid coats. "They've been such a comfort to me."

"Would you like to take them to Sardinia?"

"No, they're Cal's dogs. They belong here with him."

"You'll come back and see them often," he said, pulling her to a stop near an outcropping of rock. "In the meantime, I have something for you that might take your mind off leaving them. Consider it a promise for the future. Take off your gloves, my love."

He withdrew from his pocket a watered silk jeweler's box and opened it to reveal a solitaire diamond ring set in platinum. The fire of its many facets dazzled her. Magnificent in its classic simplicity, it left her breathless. "Where did you get it?" she gasped.

"In Vancouver. I phoned ahead to a jeweler I know of, and flew there this morning to select exactly the right engagement ring. I chose a round brilliant," he continued, slipping it on her finger, "because I knew it would look perfect on your hand. What do you think?"

She shook her head, at a loss. Where were the words to describe not just the style and quality of the gem, but the man who'd gone to so much trouble to buy it for her? "It's the most beautiful thing I've ever seen and gives me a reason to take better care of my nails from now on. You overwhelm me, Domenico." Then, thinking of the leather gloves she'd bought for him, she grimaced. "But I don't have anything to give you that comes close to matching it."

"Are you happy?"

She drew his head down and brought her mouth to his. "Perfectly!"

"That's all the gift I need."

"So happy, I'm almost afraid."

"Don't be," he said, feathering kisses along over her eyelids and down her nose. "We deserve this, Arlene, my love."

A shout from the house intruded on the moment and, looking up, they saw Cal waving and gesturing from the back door. "Something about a phone call for you, I think," Domenico said, straining to hear. "It must be important that he's calling out like that. Go ahead and see what's the matter, *cara*, and I'll get the dogs."

Slipping and sliding up the steep path, she hurried back. "What is it?" she panted, when she reached the house.

"That doctor you saw the other day just phoned," Cal said soberly. "Claims it's important you call him back before the clinic closes, seeing as how today's the last day it's open until after Christmas."

A sliver of fear pierced her bliss. Spread like poison through her body, erasing all the light and joy and leaving nothing but darkness behind. She'd been too happy. Taken too much for granted. And this was her punishment. "Oh, Cal!"

He pressed a scrap of paper into her hand. "This here's the number, missy. Better get to it and find out what's going on."

Peeling off her coat, she closeted herself in the little office off the hall and almost fell into the chair behind the desk. Her hand trembled so badly, she had to punch in the numbers twice before she made the connection, then waited an interminable thirty seconds before the nurse-receptionist put her call through.

Finally the doctor came on the line. "Your blood tests came back, Arlene," he said.

"I see." Her voice sounded high, unnatural, almost shrill. "Is there something wrong?"

"That depends."

Her heart plummeted in her chest, so close to losing its moorings that she felt sick to her stomach. Just when paradise was within her grasp, fate was stepping in to snatch it away again. "I don't know what that means."

"Among others, the lab ran a quantitative pregnancy blood test. Your results show a high hCG count—Human Chorionic Gonadotropin. The pregnancy hormone, in layman's terms."

She dropped the phone. It hit the desk with a

clatter and slithered onto her lap. Fumbling, she picked it up again. "Are you still there?" she heard him ask.

"Yes." She drew in a steadying breath. "Doctor, are you telling me I'm pregnant?"

"According to what I'm looking at here, very definitely. Didn't you suspect?"

"No," she said. "Not for a moment."

"When was your last menstrual period?"

She thought back, trying to remember. So much had happened in the last two months. "I'm not sure, although now that I think about it, I guess it must have been at the beginning of November."

"About eight weeks, then. That sounds about right. And you've shown no symptoms? No nausea, nothing like that?"

"Not really, no. As I mentioned when I came to see you, I've felt more tired than usual lately, but I put that down to overwork."

"Then I suggest you delegate for the next few months and start taking it easy. You're showing a nice healthy level of hCG, but it doesn't pay to take unnecessary chances, especially during the first trimester." He paused, then asked, "Should I be congratulating you, Arlene, or is this not good news?"

"Its…*amazing* news! Congratulations are definitely in order. But I don't understand why it was so urgent that I return your call this quickly. Are you quite certain there's nothing wrong?"

"Well, we'll schedule you for a complete checkup after the holidays, just to be sure, although I'm pretty confident everything's in order. But the party season's upon us and I wanted to give you a heads-up on alcohol. It doesn't mix well with pregnancy."

"Oh!" she said. "No, of course not."

"That's it, then. Nothing else to worry about. I'll see you next week. In the meantime, Merry Christmas!"

"You, too," she replied and, hanging up the phone, sat a moment, catching her breath and trying to wrap her mind around the news.

She was expecting a baby. Domenico's baby. And she knew exactly when she'd conceived. The only time they hadn't used protection had been in Paris on the Friday, when she'd lured Domenico back to bed in the middle of the night.

She cupped her hands over her abdomen. His baby was growing in there. All the time she'd been crying over him, reviling him, missing him, his baby had grown limbs and fingers and toes. It had ears and a dot of a nose, and if it mattered at all, a test could probably determine whether it was a girl or a boy. How could she not have known?

Still trembling, she pushed away from the desk

and went to the door. Opening it, she found Domenico and Cal stationed in the hall, waiting for her. Cal appeared haggard. Domenico's blue eyes had a bruised and hurting look to them.

He rushed forward. Gripped her arm and led her into the living room, with Cal shuffling along behind. "Tell us," he said, wrapping his arms around her. "We'll deal with it together, Arlene. The best doctors, the best treatment—whatever it takes, it's yours."

Oh, she was cruel! "Well," she said, drawing out the word until she thought Cal might smack her, "there's really not much that anyone can do to change the way things are. But I do have a Christmas gift for you, Domenico, that more or less puts your lovely diamond in the shade. But it won't be ready for a few months yet."

She stopped and smiled sweetly at both of them. "I'm pregnant."

"The hell you are!" Cal exploded, and fell into an armchair.

Domenico turned positively glassy-eyed. "Pregnant?"

"Yes," she said. "That means I'm having your baby. Sometime in August, I believe. I'll be able to give you a more accurate date after I see the doctor, next week."

Then, because she was brimming over with

more happiness than any one body could hope to contain, she started to laugh. "We're having a baby, Domenico!" she chortled. "And you, Cal, you're going to be a granddaddy!"

The next minute she was sobbing in Domenico's arms and he was whispering in her ear, thanking her, and telling her that he loved her and treasured her more than anything on earth.

The dogs picked up on the excitement and started barking. And Cal began to cry.

It took about ten minutes for everyone to settle down, although, Arlene thought, things would never be the same again, and nor would she want them to be. From that point on, they could only get better.

Domenico produced a magnum of champagne he'd brought back from Vancouver and poured a glass for Cal and himself. Cal found a bottle of sparkling grapefruit juice for Arlene. The lights on the Christmas tree sparkled in the dusk. The flames burned yellow and orange in the hearth. Outside, the snow began to fall again.

Domenico pulled Arlene close and curved a possessive arm around her waist. "To the future," he said, raising his glass. "To a new year, a wedding, and most of all to the woman who's given my life new and very real meaning. To you, Arlene, my darling one. I thank you from the bottom of my heart for trusting me to become the husband you deserve. I love you and I promise you now, with Cal as my witness, that I will treasure you for the rest of my life."

Her heart overflowing, Arlene lifted her face for his kiss. She was home at last, with the only man in the world she'd ever love.

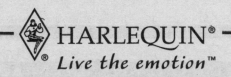

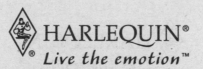

HARLEQUIN®
INTRIGUE®

BREATHTAKING ROMANTIC SUSPENSE

Shared dangers and passions lead to electrifying
romance and heart-stopping suspense!

Every month, you'll meet six new heroes
who are guaranteed to make your spine tingle
and your pulse pound. With them you'll enter
into the exciting world of Harlequin Intrigue—
where your life is on the line
and so is your heart!

THAT'S INTRIGUE—
ROMANTIC SUSPENSE
AT ITS BEST!

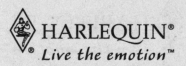

HARLEQUIN®
Live the emotion™

Harlequin® Historical
Historical Romantic Adventure!

Imagine a time of chivalrous knights and unconventional ladies, roguish rakes and impetuous heiresses, rugged cowboys and spirited frontierswomen— these rich and vivid tales will capture your imagination!

Harlequin Historical . . . they're too good to miss!

SPECIAL EDITION™

Emotional, compelling stories that capture the intensity of living, loving and creating a family in today's world.

Desire

Modern, passionate reads that are powerful and provocative.

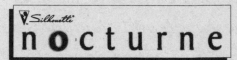

nocturne

Dramatic and sensual tales of paranormal romance.

Romantic SUSPENSE

Romances that are sparked by danger and fueled by passion.

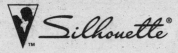

SPECIAL EDITION™

Emotional, compelling stories that capture the intensity of living, loving and creating a family in today's world.

Special Edition features bestselling authors such as Susan Mallery, Sherryl Woods, Christine Rimmer, Joan Elliott Pickart— and many more!

For a romantic, complex and emotional read, choose Silhouette Special Edition.